Belle said softly, "Okay, Pardner. Let's go."

They made their way cautiously around the side of the old house and around the corner toward the screened-in back porch. They saw it at the same time. "Uh-oh," Poppy said.

Belle spoke. "Uh-huh. Looks like this is how they got in."

Poppy crept slowly up the steps toward the door where a splintered doorjamb gave evidence of forced entry.

"Be careful, Poppy. They could be hiding on the porch."

"Okay," Poppy answered as she gingerly pulled the screen door open. "I don't think so, though. There's no vehicle here and there wouldn't have been any reason to open the gate if the perp was on foot —" Poppy lost her hold on the door handle and jumped back as a figure loomed in the doorway . . .

The Hallelujah Murders

The Hallelujah Murders

BY DOROTHY TELL

A POPPY DILLWORTH MYSTERY

The Naiad Press, Inc.
1991

Printed in the United States of America on acid-free paper
First Edition

Edited by Ann Klauda
Cover design by Pat Tong and Bonnie Liss
    (Phoenix Graphics)
Typeset by Sandi Stancil

Library of Congress Cataloging-in-Publication Data

Tell, Dorothy, 1939–
    The hallelujah murders: a Poppy Dillworth mystery / by
Dorothy Tell.
        p.   cm.
    ISBN 0-941483-88-6 : $8.95
    I. Title.
PSD3570.E518H3   1991
813'.54--dc20   91-24009
                                                        CIP

For Ruth — light of my life —
partner, lover, friend —
forever.

TABLE OF CONTENTS

Prologue   1

1   A Girl and Her Dog   5

2   Taking Sides   25

3   A Game of Cat and Mouse   47

4   Games and Players   65

5   Tom's Discovery   83

6   Fireworks   91

7   Doggone   101

8   The River Rises 111

9   Poppy Goes Fishing   123

10   Bait and Switch 137

11   Shazam!   149

Prologue

Chris Jessup sat on a limestone cliff, thirty feet above the sparkling waters of the Hermosa River. She searched her mind for some new angle she could introduce at the coming town meeting, some powerful argument for saving the river she loved. There had to be, *must* be a way to keep the dam from being built. Some way to prevent the lake that would cover even this peaceful place where she had come every day for the past year since the sudden loss of both her parents had brought her home to Texas.

She sat cross-legged and gazed intently into the red eyes of a green cicada. The large beetle-like insect just emerged from the body-husk it had inhabited for most of its seventeen years underground.

Chris had observed the insect's process for almost three hours. She had seen it emerge from the earth and climb a few feet up the trunk of the red-oak tree in whose shade she sat. The cicada stopped its upward journey, grasped the bark with its hooked feet and prepared for metamorphosis.

Chris saw it as a sign. A communication from Nature, a metaphor for her own emerging Self. It seemed that she, too, had spent all her youth in the dark, beneath the oppressive earth of her father's world. Digging, rooting her way toward the light.

How could she have been so blind? The misogynistic patriarchal church of the recently deceased Emory Zion Jessup had no place in it for ambitious women. No place even for Chris, the preacher's own daughter. Chris, who had so faithfully, until now, obeyed all her father's rules. But now there was new life, new friends. A new *world* even. The women at the camp across the river had introduced her to the Goddess. Chris felt her chest expand with new-found self-esteem as she pictured in her mind the female power of the universe.

The cicada again claimed Chris' attention as its wings unfolded, delicate and colorful in the mid-morning sunlight. Wings that had taken seventeen years to form would now carry the cicada in flight for only a few weeks. It would mate with one of the males whose shrill song vibrated against

2

Chris' eardrums like the whine of electricity. It would mate, deposit ovum and die before the winter.

A muffled barking came to Chris' ears, announcing the presence of a young girl and a dog down by the river. Every day Juno Turnbow and Kali, her Labrador retriever, would stop their morning run, and the girl would wave a greeting up to Chris.

Chris smiled and waved back, then watched as Juno and the black dog resumed their daily trek along the crude road that followed the river. The sun glinting from the dog's collar was the last thing Chris ever saw.

A shadow moved over the cicada. Strong hands brought a jagged chunk of limestone down through the air above Chris' head and hit her skull with enormous force. She slumped forward but did not fall face down because the hands then slipped beneath her arms and lifted her slight form. The killer quickly carried Chris to the edge of the cliff and released her, where her body fell head first, crashing against the layered rocks of the cliff, and tumbled into the light green pool at the bottom. A thin line of bubbles rose to the top of the water as the waves circled out and then died, claimed by the river's flow.

The killer retrieved the murder weapon and leaned against the red-oak tree, watching for a few moments, humming a tuneless dirge, waiting for the bubbles to stop.

The cicada, almost ready for flight, moved along the tree beside the killer's hand. The hand moved with lightning speed, covered the cicada with the rock and ground it into the rough bark.

3

The killer then stepped from the shadows and hurled the piece of limestone far out into the pool at the base of the cliff. It hit the water with a soft splash and settled against the rock bottom where the river began to curve into the tight loop of its Hallelujah Bend.

CHAPTER ONE
A Girl and Her Dog

Poppy Dillworth stood in the kitchen of the home in Dallas where she lived with her lover, Belle Stoner. She cocked her head, best ear out, toward the voices coming from the front of the house. Poppy knew the subject under discussion was something Belle and her daughter, Melba, would have to work out for themselves, but she felt her chest tighten as Melba's voice grew louder.

"Mother, I'm not saying you should've asked my

permission, but do you have to be so damned *evangelistic* about your new . . . er, lifestyle?"

"I don't *preach* lesbianism, Melba, though I dare say it probably would heal the minds and bodies of half the world's rest home population."

"But, *mother.* You're —"

"And the L-word is not *lifestyle* either, it's lesbian. *L-E-S-B-I-A-N.*"

"Mother, for Chrisake. Let me *talk.* You're almost seventy years old —"

"Sixty-four."

Exultant glee replaced apprehension in Poppy's chest as the voices continued. "Well, good lord, Mother. You *are* an older woman. A grandmother. Why can't you act like one?"

"Melba, sit down. You stride about like a camel. It makes me nervous. Now listen to me. I am acting like a grandmother. Are you questioning my love for your children? Or for *you?*"

"Oh no, Mother. It's not that. I know you love us, it's just that — Well, it's Ron. He . . . *you* know how he is. He's so damn conscious of his *image,* especially right now during the budget session. You know how shaky city jobs are."

"Well, my son-in-law Ronald, the father of my *beloved* grandchildren, would probably be the first one to promote the myth that old women are ineffectual and useless. And, Melba, as *you* have so succinctly pointed out, *I* fall into that category. So how can an old woman's living arrangements possibly affect the livelihood of a young, virile, college-educated, Caucasian male?"

Poppy's inner voice entered the fray. *Attagirl,*

Belle. Now follow that left hook to the prejudice with an uppercut to the bias.

The wall phone beside her ear whirred loudly. Poppy jumped and reached for it. *Whatever happened to phones that ring? Ring-ring-ring, not whirtle-whirtle.*

"Hello, Dillworth here."

Poppy quickly sobered as she listened to the breathless voice rattling into her hear. "Slow down, Lovey," Poppy said. "I didn't get all that. Whoa. Stop. I can't understand a word . . . Have you got your teeth in? Well, take a deep breath and start over."

After a pause punctuated by wet-sounding clacks, the voice began anew, the words more distinct now. "I *said* there's some skullduggery goin' on down here. Yesterday afternoon Juno, you know, Lil's daughter? Well she —"

Poppy interrupted. "Lovely, suck it up, girl. Of course I know who Lil's daughter is. Irma and I were down there when the girl was born. What's the matter with you anyway? Old age put your brain on hold?"

"Dillworth, you asshole. Shut up and listen. This is serious stuff."

Poppy caught a note of something besides anxiety in her old friend's voice. Something like the edges of a deep sadness. She sobered immediately and said, "Uh, okay . . ."

Silence lengthened at Lovey's end of the line. Poppy barked at the phone. "Well? Go for it. It's your nickel."

"Well, Juno was down by the river with her dog

7

and she saw somebody under the water in that long pool they call the Font. You know. Where they used to do the dunking after the revivals? Well, Juno jumped right in, spunky kid, and pulled her out —"

Poppy broke in. "Her *who?* Who was it? Is Juno all right?"

"Yeah, Juno's all right. A little shook up, though." Lovey's voice faltered for a second as she continued. "It was the preacher's daughter, Chris Jessup, that was in the water and she was dead. I been taking care of the livestock and the orchards for Chris since her folks were killed last year. Sort of got to know her . . . she was a real sweet kid . . . Me 'n Pete 'n Lil talked it over and we think you oughta come on down here for a while and see if you can get to the bottom of this mess. See, the county coroner has ruled the death was accidental drowning, but Chris has been crawling around on those rocks and swimming in that pool most every day since early spring, and we don't think it was an accident. Besides, this damn dam thing has divided the whole county and there's bad feelings all around."

"Lovey, why do you think she was murdered?"

"Because she was beginning to change a lot of folks' minds about damming up the river."

"Yeah. I see what you mean," Poppy said, then asked, "When's the funeral?"

"Tomorrow."

"Hmm . . . well, I sure think I'd like to know some more about this whole thing. Besides, there's someone I want y'all to meet. I've got a new partner. Her name is Belle Stoner."

Poppy waited for the impact of her news to hit

8

her old friend. Finally Lovey spoke. "Belle Starr, you say? Does she wear guns?"

Poppy grinned and her face softened as she answered, "It's Stoner, not Starr, and she doesn't have to wear guns. Just the sight of her knocks *me* out."

Silence again from Lovey. Long silence. "Oh, I see. She's more than just your business partner then, I reckon?"

"Yeah, Lovey. A whole lot more."

". . . Well, I can't promise how Pete's gonna react to all this. You know she thinks Irma hung the moon."

"Yeah. I do, too, but Irma's been gone for quite a while now, and my life was pretty bleak. You're going to love Belle. Pete will, too. You'll see . . . Listen, Lovey, we'll be down there just as soon as we find someone to cat-sit."

"A *cat! You* have a *cat?*"

Poppy went to find Belle, who had left the room halfway through Poppy's phone conversation with T.J. Ballew, the woman who sometimes acted as an operative for Poppy's detective agency. Belle threw suitcases on the bed and asked, "How long will we be gone?"

"Don't know. Better take enough for a couple of weeks. Lovey says the river level's down right now because of the dry weather. The cabins are empty so we'll get one all to ourselves. We might even get in a little fishing." Poppy cut her clear blue eyes up to Belle's face, watching her over the top of her glasses.

Belle grinned and raised her eyebrows. "Is this just a ruse to get to go fishing, Papillon?"

"No, honey. This is for real." Poppy suppressed a

9

little shudder as she recalled the very real urgency in Lovey's voice. She remembered past springtimes and canoeing down the wild stretch of river they would soon see. She hoped that snagging a feisty bass from one of its deep pools would be the most excitement they would experience.

The short trip south from Dallas down State Highway 67 took Poppy and Belle through country that changed rapidly from flat, black land and red hills covered with oak, cottonwood and pecan trees. The last day of June was hot and clear and the sun shone hard against the small towns nestled by the roadside, showing their unkempt backsides to the highway that had passed them by. Mobile homes crowded in like abandoned boxcars below the elevated ribbon of asphalt that carried them across the red Brazos River. The highway took them into the limestone hills where the Hermosa River circled back on itself, curling like a lazy snake through Pecan Valley, the oldest town in Hermosa County.

About a mile outside of town, Poppy wheeled the royal blue Isuzu Trooper off the main road and beneath a hanging weathered sign:

Hallelujah Bend Women's Camp — Est. 1935
For Sale
Pecans, Catfish, Herbs, Fruit & Vegetables in Season
Honk at Gate for Service.

Stands of tall oaks, pecans and walnuts rose on either side of the sandy road that led to the main house. The trees gave way abruptly to a large clearing that was filled to the edge of the road with a garden. Corn and tomatoes in rows as straight and neat as corduroy marched off to the far trees.

A stooped old woman in pink shorts, a pink shirt and a straw hat guided a plow pulled by an aged white mule. The woman waved her hat in the direction of the vehicle but made no effort to slow the mule. Poppy watched in admiration for a moment, then beeped the horn in greeting.

"Lovey never changes," Poppy said to Belle. "I wonder how old she is now? Got to be seventy-five at least. Maybe older. She was one of the camp's first permanent residents, you know, back in the thirties when old Patty Bett Turnbow opened the camp. Whatta girl. She's the one I was telling you about who's working on the *Cronesnest* project, the retirement home for old women." Poppy's knees, aching from the drive from Dallas, reminded her of her own advancing age. *Yeppers — I betcha Lovey and me together are keeping Ben-Gay's profits healthy.*

Poppy glanced at Belle, who had wound her long single braid around her head and was now securing it with pins. She and Belle had been together only six months now, but Poppy already recognized this action as an indication of Belle's nervousness at meeting Poppy's old friends. Poppy had secretly dubbed it the Brunhilde hairdo, Belle's little Viking shield against the unknown.

Poppy's heart swelled as it always did when she looked at her lover, the woman whose very presence in her life still seemed like a miracle. All those long happy years with Irma and then the period of

11

devastating loneliness after Irma's death . . . To have found love again — at this age — *had* to be a miracle. *You must still have something going for you, Wondercrone, else that marvelous woman wouldn't stay around.*

Belle interrupted Poppy's inner musings. "I hope Chris Jessup wasn't really murdered, Poppy. What do you think?" She turned worried brown eyes toward Poppy as she unhooked her seatbelt.

"Well, I —" The rest of Poppy's words were drowned out by the barking of a large black dog who dashed frantically back and forth across the road just beyond an open metal gate. "Good old Kali." Poppy's heart gladdened at the prospect of petting the big dog.

She let the Trooper roll slowly to a stop in front of an old-fashioned farmhouse. *Holey moley, what a color.* Poppy gazed at the new, bright lavender paint job on the house and porch. *Either Pete finally caught up with the psychedelic sixties or Lovey found a sale on purple paint.* She didn't think that Lil, a wood sculptor with good sense and fairly good taste, would have had anything to do with the apparition in front of them.

A young girl appeared from behind the house and subdued the excited dog. She smiled shyly at the women in the vehicle. Hot dry air rushed over Poppy as she rolled down her window. "Hi, Junebug. Where's your Mom? She up at the studio?"

"No ma'am. She's down by the river. She's pretty worried about what happened to Miss Jessup. She and Marsha went down there to see if they could figure out what really *did* happen." Juno wiped a hand across her forehead, clearing perspiration from her eyes, then dried her hand on the frayed leg of her denim cutoffs. Astride the panting dog, she clasped its sides tightly with her knees, holding its leather collar with her free hand.

Something did a little leprechaun skip in Poppy's heart as she gazed into the soft brown eyes of the black dog. She swallowed against the sudden constriction in her throat that always happened when she remembered how much she missed old Ellie, her springer spaniel who had died a year or so ago. *Come on, Dillworth. Get it together. A damn dog would just dig up the yard . . . probably eat Cleo. Maybe cause a divorce. We gotta job to do here. Suck it up, girl.*

Aloud she said, "Why don't you hop in, Junebug, and we'll go down by the river and find your mom and Marsha. We need to get a look at the scene anyway."

Belle pressed a hand over Poppy's arm and spoke gently to the girl who still straddled the black dog. "How do you feel about going back down there, dear? Will that be a problem for you? Is it okay with your mother?"

Juno straightened and drew up her shoulders. Her blue eyes widened as she answered, "Oh, it's okay with Mom. It was mostly scary *after* it happened. When I remember about it. You know. About Miss Jessup being dead, I mean."

Poppy reached behind her and opened the door. "Climb in, sugar, but you'd better leave Kali here. She —"

Belle interrupted. "No, no. Bring her." She squeezed Poppy's arm. "Bad business, separating a girl from her dog."

13

Poppy grinned at Juno and nodded, then cut her eyes toward Belle, who sat smugly demure, looking straight ahead as a beaming Juno let Kali into the back seat. *Hmmm, Dillworth. Whaddaya think she meant by that? Think she knows how much you want a dog?* Poppy glanced up into the rearview mirror at the reflection of Juno's happy face. *Well, whatever she meant, Belle's made her first conquest here, that's for sure.*

Poppy slapped the heel of her hand against her head. "Well. Please forgive my bad manners. Juno, this lady here is my new friend, Belle Stoner . . . Belle, this young'un is my old friend, Juno May Turnbow." Poppy watched in the mirror as Belle turned in the seat to face Juno and extended her hand.

Juno took Belle's hand and shook it soberly. "Are you Poppy's lifemate like Irma was?"

To Poppy's admiration, Belle didn't miss a beat as she answered the precocious question with respectful sincerity. "Well . . . I could never take Irma's place in Poppy's heart, Juno. But, thank goodness, Poppy's heart is big enough so I can have a place in it all my own. If you mean, do I love Poppy and want to spend the rest of my life with her, the answer is yes."

Poppy cleared her throat and busied herself with keeping the Trooper on the rough road. Tears had formed in the corners of her eyes and she knuckled them away. "Dang cedar pollen," she muttered.

They rode in silence through dense woods of pecan and cottonwood trees. The noon sun shafted through the green canopy over their heads, splashing the sandy lane with light. The woods soon gave way to a clearing where a cluster of neat log cabins surrounded a cement-floored pavilion. Blue and white parachute fabric hung from a tall center pole and fluttered limply in the light breeze. The chutes formed a canopy of shade for the pavilion when they were attached to the front roof-peak of each surrounding cabin. It always reminded Poppy of the jousting fields in the movie, *Camelot*. But the only combatants in the lists today were a pair of fox squirrels chattering in the shade of a towering native pecan tree.

The first time Poppy had come to the women's camp was the summer she and Irma became lovers. That was forty-odd summers ago, when the world was trying to put itself back together after the second great war. She had returned many times, but the visit which came to mind now was the time three summers back, the year after Irma died. The black pain of that time settled briefly in Poppy's abdomen, a nauseating, momentary loss of emotional balance, a searing memory of her friends pleading with her to go on with life, to pull out of her deep depression.

She braked the Trooper to a stop and, without speaking, quickly got out and walked away from Belle and her young friend. She had to rid herself of the sudden need to cry, to release a part of her grief that had remained hidden until now. She stood for a moment, breathing deeply, using the time Belle and Juno had wordlessly given her to regain her composure. She dried her eyes on her shirt sleeve and yanked hard on the bell rope hanging beside the center pole of the pavilion. Three rings, then a short silence, and then three more loud peals resounded across the meadow, the sound finally swallowed by the high whine of cicadas.

A distant answering *halloo* came from the direction of the river, then in a moment three beeps of a horn. Soon a plume of dust rose into the hot air and began to move toward them. Kali leaped from the vehicle and bolted down the road toward the champagne-pink Continental that hove into view, a sparkling mirage shimmering like a cruise ship on a sea of heat waves.

The sleek automobile stopped beside the boxy Isuzu and Lil Turnbow disembarked from the passenger side. She ran a big square hand through close-cropped waves of hair that was just beginning to gray. She then stood still, obviously waiting for Poppy to make a move. Poppy grinned and opened her arms to receive the bone-crunching hug she knew was coming.

"Still rasslin' those logs around, I see." Poppy laughed as she extricated herself from the sturdy woman's grasp.

Over Lil's shoulder, Poppy caught her first sight of the fabled Marsha. Ex-Miss Texas, still drop-dead beautiful at forty-seven, widow of Senator Thomas Needham. She had the kind of natural red hair that glows with silver glints when its owner begins to age . . . and a body Cher would envy. Lil stepped back swiftly and said, "Poppy, this is Marsha."

Marsha Needham flashed a zillion-dollar smile at Poppy and stepped forward for *her* hug. Poppy's ears flamed as she rose on her toes and gingerly hugged the taller woman. She turned quickly, locating Belle close behind her. "Harumph," she began. "Um, Marsha, this is my partner, Belle Stoner. Belle,

Marsha Needham." Poppy became aware of Lil grinning at her from where she leaned against the fender of the Continental. "Oh-hey, Belle. This joker is Lil Turnbow, Juno's mother. Also known as Paulette Bunyan by the locals."

Poppy gave Belle a chance to nod and smile, then she turned brusquely to the business she was there to do. "Let's get on down to the river so Belle and I can take some videotape of the scene. Besides, this heat's taking my breath away."

Poppy and Belle, with Juno and Kali again in the back seat, followed the Continental as it crept slowly down the road to the river. Poppy registered the fact that now very little dust rose from beneath the big tires on the vehicle in front of them. She was also painfully aware that this considerate action by the driver surprised her. Which meant that Poppy had once again allowed herself to form an opinion of someone without really knowing her. Not a good habit for a private eye to have. She would work on it.

They had driven less than a hundred yards when the forest thinned and the road disappeared into a large sandy beach that dipped steeply toward the clear, green river. On the far side, limestone cliffs rose in white and gray layers high above a long curving pool. A line of bushy treetops marched away from the lip of the cliff where a lone oak grew apart from the rest, spreading its dark shadow down the rocky cliff face and into the water below.

They stopped the vehicles short of the sandy river bank. Poppy quickly prepared her video camera for use, positioned it against her shoulder and began to record the scene before her. She stopped and turned to her old friend. "Lil, would it be okay if Juno helps me for a few minutes? Shows me where she found Chris and tells me all about it?"

Juno, who had been standing snuggled beneath Lil's strong arm, turned up her face inquiringly. "Can I, Mom? I really feel okay about it. Besides —" She looked evenly at Poppy. "Poppy needs my help. Me and Kali are the only ones who know how it really was."

Lil smiled down at her daughter and clasped her firmly to her, wrapping her muscular arms tightly around the girl's slight shoulders. Pride showed in the set of her jaw as she released her. "All right, honey. I'll be close by in case you need a hug." Juno's chin came up sharply. Lil raised her hands defensively. "Or a Band-Aid, or money. Or, you know, any of that stuff a mom's good for."

Juno grinned and stepped toward Poppy and Belle, obviously ready to discharge her obligations to the adult world without any more ado.

Poppy listened raptly as Juno began speaking, then interrupted. "Can you speak up, Junebug? Talk louder so this machine can hear you?"

Juno began again. "It was Thursday morning, about ten-thirty, when Kali and me passed by on the path over there where the cars are parked."

Poppy filmed the area Juno pointed to, then asked, "Do you remember how the area looked? Anything unusual around?

"Umm . . . no. I don't remember anything different. I was catching grasshoppers to use for bait. I almost didn't remember to wave at Miss Jessup. But when I looked up there —" she pointed to the

18

area where the big oak stood sentinel atop the cliff. "She was sitting there just like always. I waved to her and she waved back."

Poppy pointed the camera at the indicated area and continued to record both picture and voice as Juno resumed her story.

"After I waved, Kali jumped a jumbo and we chased it off yonder down the road." Again she pointed, and Poppy followed the motion with the quietly whirring camera. "We'd only gotten a little ways past the bend when Kali started whining and trotted back this way. I followed her back here to the place where the cars are. She stood there real still for a second and looked at the water, then she ran and jumped in. It was then I saw what looked like somebody in the water. I ran down to the edge and waded in. As I got closer I could see it was Miss Jessup. I went under and got hold of her hair and pulled her up to the shallows. I dragged her up to where her head was out of the water on the sand. I got scared 'cause she wasn't moving or anything. That's when I saw there was blood on her head."

Juno's eyes widened at the memory and she hugged her arms across her stomach. Poppy noted a little tremble in the girl's voice as she continued. "I wanted to make her breathe again, but I didn't know how. Besides —" She cast her eyes down, then up at Poppy. "I knew Miss Jessup was dead, Poppy. I mean, I've seen dead things before. I wanted to put something over her face, but I didn't have anything. So I ran back to the house to find Mom or somebody to help."

Lil, who hadn't been far away, moved closer and placed a protective arm gently around Juno's shoulders.

Belle spoke up. "Who did you find, Juno? Who came back with you?"

"Pete was down at the catfish ponds. She said she heard me screechin' like a banshee and caught up with me in the Ark." Poppy barely suppressed a smile at the thought of her old friend, Odessa "Pete" Peters, coming to the rescue in her 1952 Ford truck that was so old and rickety, wired-up, modified and paintless that it had been dubbed the "Ark" by Irma at least twenty years ago.

Juno continued, "Pete sent me on to the house and she went down to the river to see if she could help Miss Jessup. I *told* Pete she was dead, but she didn't believe me."

Poppy broke in. "Wait a minute. You say Pete *heard* you? Pete can't even hear herself toot."

Juno giggled and shook her head. "She got her a new hearing aid and she says now she can even hear the catfish meow when she feeds 'em." Juno's smile faded as she continued. "Mom was gone when I got to the house and Lovey musta been down by the gardens, so I called the Sheriff's office in town and told the dispatcher lady what happened."

Poppy looked up from the eyepiece of the camera in surprised admiration. "What happened then?" She dropped her eye to the viewfinder again, moving it slightly to relocate Juno's face.

"Well. After she asked me a bunch of questions, they sent the ambulance out here. By that time Mom was back from the post office and we met the ambulance at the gate and led the driver down here to the river."

Poppy moved the camera away from Juno and up until it framed Lil's head and shoulders. "Lil, you have anything to add to Junebug's story?"

"Not really. Except I knew from the first they were going to call it an accident. Sheriff Gatling kept asking questions like, 'what time did Juno think it was when Miss Jessup *fell* off the cliff?' or 'did Juno hear the splash when Miss Jessup *fell* in?' Nothing to indicate he was even going to *look* for evidence of foul play."

Poppy adjusted her glasses and dabbed her perspiring face with a faded purple bandanna. "You seem pretty certain Chris Jessup was murdered, Lil. What do you base that on?"

"Well, for one thing, Chris had pretty much stirred up a hornet's nest since she threw herself into the fight against the dam. There are some pretty powerful people hereabouts who'll probably celebrate after she's put in the ground tomorrow." Lil's gaze flickered past Poppy toward Marsha as she continued. "There's a lot of folks not speaking to each other any more . . . Even within families." She moved her gaze back to Poppy. "Chris was using what was left of her daddy's influence to bring attention to all the hurrah going on about damming the Hermosa . . . and she was beginning to make a difference, too. With the election less than three weeks away . . . Chris just had a way about her, Poppy. She was changing people's minds. I was beginning to think we had a real chance to save the river."

Lil paused and looked around at the river and the forest beyond, then turned back to Poppy. "This land has been in my family for about a hundred and fifty years . . . ever since Texas was a Republic. And the women's camp is an important part of lesbian culture. When my great-aunt Patti Bett started it as a place for women back during the depression, I don't think even *she* knew what it would come to mean. We've just *got* to find a way to save it."

Poppy noticed Lil's eyes had begun to shine with unshed tears. Marsha slipped her arm through Lil's and leaned close to her. Lil folded her fingers around Marsha's arm, then squared her shoulders and continued.

"I think somebody pushed her off that cliff into the river, Poppy. I don't think she fell. She'd been swimming down here every day the weather would allow since early spring." Lil turned her gaze toward the tree on the cliff. "I just really believe she was murdered. And that's that."

Poppy saw a black blur shoot past Lil's shoulder toward the river, flashing drops of water sprayed in every direction as Kali hit the water chasing after a stick Juno had tossed far out into the pool. Memories pressed in close and Poppy's throat tightened as she watched Juno take the retrieved stick from the dog's mouth. Juno fell laughing into the sand as Kali's exuberant dance knocked her off balance. The dog stood over the girl and shook water from her coat in a shining cloud of spray.

Lil shouted, "Oh no, Juno! What a mess. You two'll have to walk back."

Belle spoke. "We wouldn't hear of it." She cast a

look toward Poppy. "Would we, Papillon? As far as I know, that's what back seats are for."

Poppy cleared her throat and nodded in happy agreement. Satisfied with her morning's work, she pressed the power button on the video camera, and lowered it from her aching shoulder. She massaged her right elbow with the fingers of her left hand as she spoke. "Thanks, Lil." She turned to Juno. "You too, honey. Thanks for helping us."

To Belle she said, "Tomorrow morning we'll see if Pete and Lovey will ride into town with us to the funeral. On the way we can stop off up there on the Jessup side of the river and take a look around that tree, get that area on tape too. Sometimes this camera sees things I'm prone to miss."

CHAPTER TWO
Taking Sides

The next day was clear and blue and turned out to be a classic Texas July first. No clouds offered shadows for escaping the burning noon sunshine. The dark green leaves of the oak and pecan trees curled in on themselves, preserving what moisture they could, and the landscape shimmered in the windless heat, dry and drooping under a veil of fine white dust.

Poppy glanced at Belle who stood beside her on

the high bluff above the river where Chris Jessup had sat the last time she waved to Juno. The last twenty-four uncomfortable hours that they had spent with Poppy's old friends had been worse than Poppy had expected. Even though warned of Pete's inability to accept Belle as Poppy's new lover, Poppy had not really been prepared for Pete's curmudgeonly behavior. She looked back over her shoulder at where the Trooper was parked, engine and air conditioner running. Pete sat stolidly beside Lovey on the back seat, her battered felt fedora pulled down over her eyes and her arms crossed stubbornly across her middle. Poppy's inner voice grumbled in exasperation. *Mean-tempered old geezer. Good dose of stewed prunes probably do that woman some good.*

Belle delicately cleared her throat. "Poppy . . . honey. Don't worry about it. I'm okay. And Pete'll come around sooner or later. Let's give her a chance to get used to the idea. Right now we've got some work to do with the camera, and then we need to get on into town for the funeral."

Poppy nodded agreement and positioned the video camera against her shoulder. "Belle, tell me your impressions of this place while I film it . . . please." She stepped out of the shade and powered on the camera.

"Umm, okay. We're standing on top of a bluff in the shade of an oak tree. The river down below is running only a small trickle between long clear pools. From here I can see the women's camp across the river and behind us I can see the Jessup place that Lovey pointed out. The Springs, she called it, where Chris Jessup lived. There must be a highway, or road, between us and the Springs, because I can see light glinting from something moving."

Poppy moved the camera to take in all the area of Belle's description and then stepped away from the tree and moved closer to the lip of the dropoff. Glare from the white limestone of the riverbed caused her to squint as she panned the pool where Chris Jessup had been found.

"Look here, Poppy. There's some kind of light-colored smudge on the tree over here." Belle bent and leaned forward until her face was only inches from the tree. "Come over here, Poppy. There's something mashed down in the cracks of the bark, but I can't make out what it is."

Poppy turned the camera toward the tree and zoomed in for a close-up of the area indicated by Belle's finger. Then she lowered the camera and dug a small Bausch & Lomb collapsible magnifying glass from her pocket. She spread the two lenses, centering them, one over the other, to get the most enlargement she could. "I see something too, hon. It looks like some kind of bug wing or something . . . here, hold this thing —" She held out the camera. "While I scrape some of this buggie into a baggie."

Even though the day was hot and airless, Poppy savored the intimate warmth of Belle's body against hers as Belle leaned in close to watch her. She picked gingerly at the tree bark with her small, pearl-handled pocket knife, flaking tiny bits of material into a Ziploc sandwich bag. A disconcerting rush of wanting gathered in Poppy's groin as Belle pressed closer. She slid her arm around Belle's slim waist and pulled her around the tree until they were out of sight of the two women who sat waiting in the vehicle.

The vehement suddenness of her physical need surprised Poppy into action. She pressed Belle against the tree and covered her soft mouth with kisses that grew into quick passionate gasps as Belle began to move her hips rhythmically.

"Oh, Papillon . . . oh, sweetheart." Belle breathed harsh little puffs against Poppy's neck as Poppy slipped her hand inside the waistband of Belle's skirt and then down to find her center. She circled her long fingers over Belle's smooth abdomen and fluttered them against her soft vulva. "Oh, Poppy . . . I love you, love you, *love* you!" Belle clasped Poppy in a fierce embrace.

The pulse of Poppy's passion pounded in her ears, but the heat of the day and the pain in her knees made it perfectly clear that she would have to finish what she had started when she was flat on her back. On a bed. Away from the all-seeing eye of the noontime sun.

Beee-eeep — beep — beep . . . beee-eee-eeep!

Poppy jumped from Belle's arms as if she had been shot. "Shit." She felt an embarrassed flush heat up her ears.

"Shhh!"

"Well, hell, Belle. It's your fault, you shameless hussy. You'd make a woman forget her own hangin'." She grinned down at Belle, who was straightening her clothing and brushing away bits of tree bark.

Belle smiled up at Poppy, her brown eyes larger than usual. "That's all right, honey. It'll keep. Come on. Let's get back to your friends. If Pete figures out what we've been up to, she's likely to *walk* to town or something. Do I look okay?"

Poppy nodded soberly. "You look fine." *Fine? That's a very short word, Wondercrone. How about "wonderful?" Or "marvelous?" Or — "best looking woman in the world?" Or "fiery wanton temptress?" Or how about "The light of your life," you tongue-tied old toad!*

Amid the continuing castigations of her inner voice, Poppy followed Belle back to the Trooper, berating herself for being unable to verbally express the fullness of her emotions. She watched Belle get into the vehicle while she loaded the camera and tucked away her bag of scrapings.

She took a deep breath, squared her shoulders and entered the cool, grim silence where three women sat staring straight ahead. Her lips puckered into a silent whistle. A tune came to mind. She couldn't help it. She grinned into the rearview mirror at the turned-down brim of Pete's fedora and let the whistle rise to an audible level. *If you go down to the woods today . . . you're in for a big surprise . . . 'cause this is the day when teddy-bears have their pickkk-nickkk.*

They drove from the bluff to Pecan Valley over country roads that brought them onto the State Highway, then off the highway again just after they crossed the Hermosa River. The town hadn't changed much since the nineteen-hundreds. Large two- and three-story Victorian houses sat back from the tree-lined streets on deep sloping yards. The houses soon gave way to old brick and newer cement-block commercial buildings which crowded together along the streets that formed the town square. In the center of a neatly trimmed lawn, a white-domed limestone courthouse rose above its lower floors of pink marble like a strawberry shortcake in a square, green bowl.

Lovey directed the way to the post office and Poppy double-parked while Belle went in to Express-mail the specimen taken from the tree to Delbert Swindell. Delbert, or Bubba, as everyone knew him, had recently taken a job as an instructor at a police academy in Dallas and he owed Poppy a favor. She figured to collect by asking him to analyze the scrapings from the tree bark. When Belle returned they resumed following Lovey's directions through Pecan Valley.

Poppy thought the town seemed oddly quiet for a Saturday. Then she remembered the funeral, the other reason they had braved the oppressive heat of this day.

Pete spoke her first word since breakfast. "Yonder." She jabbed Poppy's shoulder with a gnarled index finger and pointed ahead at a white spire rising from a grove of pecan trees. "That's it. But it's too early to go in. Dunno why we had to get here so blamed early, Dillworth."

Poppy backed the Isuzu into a shady corner parking place close to the front of the church lot, where she had an unobstructed view of both the front drive and the awning-covered walkway that led to and then up the wide steps of the venerable old church. She glanced at Pete's reflection in the mirror. Pete's thin mouth was turned sullenly down in the corners.

"I need your help, Pete . . ." Poppy turned in the seat and included her other friend in the conversation. "You, too, Lovey. You women know everyone in this town. I need you to identify folks for me as they go in the church. Memory sometimes fails me . . . but —" She tapped the video camera Belle had just handed her. "This thing here doesn't miss a trick. *And* I can see it over and over again any time I want to. If it hadn't been for this camera's eye, a young Deputy Sheriff I know wouldn't be around to send out birth announcements this fall."

"Humph," Pete grunted. "Well, get it turned on, Sherlock, 'cause yonder comes two hyenas you oughta get some pictures of." She pointed across the lot where a black and white county Ford sedan had pulled up. The sun glinted dully through the red and blue light bar on its roof as Poppy adjusted her eye to the camera.

A tall, slope-shouldered man of about thirty got out, hitching up what Poppy was sure was a shoulder holster strap. He straightened and raised both hands carefully to adjust his tan western-style hat, exposing the flash of what looked like a Sheriff's badge. Smoothing his lapels, he started around the car toward the passenger side.

Pete spoke, her quavery voice rich with sarcasm. "That there is Troy Gatling, our suck-egg Sheriff."

The passenger door opened just as the Sheriff reached for it and a shapely leg encased in black lace hosiery emerged, followed immediately by the rest of a Dolly Parton clone dressed in a form-fitting

31

black suit with a decolletage so daring it left Poppy a little breathless. Even Belle breathed an appreciative sigh.

Pete continued in a derisive tone, "The owner of them hooters is Lavon Gatling. Miz pro-lake of Pecan Valley. She buys and sells real estate . . . when she ain't on her back, that is. Folks hereabouts call her Gunner."

Gunner Gatling? Well, well, Wondercrone. At least folks in Pecan Valley have a sense of humor.

Lovey chimed in. "Shame on you, Odessa Peters. You know good and well if you were twenty years younger, you'd be lining up for a chance to plant your nose between those hooters yourself!"

Poppy couldn't be quite sure because her eye was still glued to the camera viewfinder, but she could swear she *felt* Pete grin a little.

"And besides," Lovey continued, "Gunner may spend a lot of time in the sack, but she's not *dumb*. Nosiree. Not by a long shot. She plays these good ole boys like they were pieces on a chessboard. She's got a good half of 'em believing they'll live the life of Riley on their water-starved little farms if they help her dam up our river. And I know for a *fact* she's got a thing for the ladies, Poppy."

Poppy pressed the close-up button as she followed the progress of the Sheriff and his blonde wife up the church steps. She realized she had zoomed in and focused right on Lavon Gatling's undulating, black-clad bottom but it was too late to change course.

Belle supplied the appropriate sound track with a suggestive, "Boomchick-boomchicka-boom-boom-boom."

Poppy cleared her throat, lowering the camera as the Gatlings entered the church. She turned to look at Lovey. "How do you know any such a personal thing about that woman, Lovey? Gunner Gatling been puttin' the eye on you?"

Lovey pressed her lips together and sucked reprovingly against her teeth. "No. You idjut . . . but I was out by the studio well-house one day when Gunner came to call on Lil about the lake business. It wasn't five minutes till she was wrapped around Lil like a python. Right out there on the porch, too. Lil didn't fight her off either. It was back before Lil and Marsha got thick, see. Anyway, they went inside and didn't come out for near an hour. For a while there it was better'n being parked outside a cheap motel . . . all the squealing and carrying on."

Pete turned her head slowly like an old turtle and snapped at Lovey, "How's come you didn't tell me about that?"

Lovey's lashes flickered down and the corners of her mouth came up in a soft smile. "Well . . . you knew about it. Sort of."

"Didn't." Pete stuck her chin out.

"You remember the last time we had a wine and candlelight dinner? And afterwards?"

"Yes . . . I 'member *that*. Haven't gone plumb dotty, you know. But what's that got to do with Gunner?"

"Well, Petey. I guess listening to those girls having so much fun kinda put me in the mood." Lovey grinned mischievously at her lover.

"Oh."

Poppy noted with suppressed glee that the part of Pete's face showing under her hat began to glow a rosy pink.

Cars and pickups began to fill the lot and people filed steadily up the steps. Lovey and Pete pointed to and named them all, being sure to identify each one as either pro-lake or pro-river according to his or her stand on the issue that divided the inhabitants of Pecan Valley and surrounding Hermosa County. But there were no more *principals,* as Poppy had labelled them in her mind, until Pete jabbed her shoulder again and pointed toward the trees beside the church.

"Here comes the Needhams . . . yonder. Comin' across the grass."

Poppy turned the camera on the group of dark-clad people making their way along a path that led from the shady sidewalks across the bright green lawn. A tall red-haired man and an equally tall red-haired woman, obviously parents of the two lanky auburn-haired young women behind them, stepped in a peculiarly stiff marching rhythm, their gaze even and straight ahead. The ungraceful way, Poppy thought, that people move on foot when they suddenly find themselves outside the secure cocoons of automobiles and have to actually *walk* somewhere.

"Uh-oh," said Pete, as she jerked a thumb in the direction of the street. "Here comes Lil and Marsha."

Poppy wanted to look where Pete pointed, but her eye was pressed to the viewfinder. The smooth cadence of the people walking across the lawns had suddenly disintegrated into a stuttering half-step. An expression of dismay edged with distaste flickered across the face of the tall woman. She squared her shoulders, slid her hand over the crook of the man's elbow and resumed her dogged march toward the church.

Lovey said, "It's okay. Lil must've seen 'em. She's driving around the block."

Poppy asked, "Which one of those carrot-tops is Marsha related to . . . and what's the conflict?" *Attagirl, Wondercrone. The conflict ought to be clear to anyone with eyes and ears. The senator's widow takes a lover — and she's a rantin'-ravin' radical-feminist, river-lovin' lesbian!*

"Marsha is Gloria Needham's sister. Marsha and Glo married the Needham brothers, Thomas and Ty. Everyone 'round here thought it was the cutest thing since rumble-seats . . . how all those red-heads got together. Inseparable as kids. Never saw one that you didn't see all four."

"Humph. Cute," Pete interrupted. "Well, it ain't so cute any more, now that Marsha spends all her time out at the camp. See Poppy —" Pete poked Poppy's arm for emphasis. "Ty Needham is *the* banker in Pecan Valley. Him and Glo are the social scene here. They ain't *in* it. They *are* it. And them two girls yonder —" Pete pointed toward the church doorway where Tyrone Needham held the door for his wife and daughters. "They don't want for nothin'. They both go to S.M.U. up in Dallas and I figure what they spend on clothes alone would keep the camp running."

Lovey added, "Marsha used to be a big part of all that kind of highlife, too, before she fell for Lil. There was already a split in the county because of the lake-river controversy, but when folks got wind of Marsha's new sexual preference . . . Well. Marsha and Glo haven't spoken to one another since the last town meeting. And *that* was mostly shouting."

Belle punched Poppy's leg and motioned toward the street that led from the town square up to the church. "Here comes Lil and Marsha."

Poppy swung the camera and focused on the long, pink Lincoln that had just backed into a parking space in the far corner of the lot. The back door opened just as the wheels quit rolling and Juno Turnbow emerged, looking uncomfortable and stiff in a sedate blue dress. Poppy realized it was the first time she had ever seen the girl in anything except shorts or jeans. Lil Turnbow stepped from the driver's side into the sunlight. She wore a mid-calf length, full skirt that swirled around her lower calves as she tugged at the waistband. A long Bea Arthur vest of aquamarine partially covered her sturdy torso and her tailored white shirt. No-nonsense, spool-heeled pumps completed her attire.

"She sure dresses better since Marsha's been coming around," said Lovey.

"Humph," Pete snorted. "I think she looks like a prissy-tail *fluff* in that skirt."

Belle tittered and Poppy nudged her with a toe. *Yeah, W.C.,* Poppy's inner voice agreed with Pete. *Kinda like a bouquet on a vinegar barrel.*

Lovey said, "She's just learning to celebrate her femininity, Pete."

Pete sulked, her arms crossed tight over her middle. "Well, *I* think it's plumb *queer,* that's what."

"Shush, you. Nasty-mouthed old grump." Lovey puckered her lips reprovingly at Pete.

Poppy felt Belle's leg shaking with silent laughter.

Marsha Needham stepped into view around the end of the long car. Belle murmured in appreciation. "Now, there's a sight."

Poppy silently agreed as she filmed the two women and the girl walking slowly toward them. Marsha was dressed in a sea-green silk shirt-dress that alternately clung to, then swished past, her long legs. Poppy couldn't resist asking, "Does she always walk like she's coming down a pageant runway?"

Pete answered, with just a bit of awe, Poppy thought. "Yep. Just like a racehorse. Ain't she elegant?"

"Why, Pete. Don't tell me you've gone and become a groupie." Poppy laughed at her old friend's fervor.

"C'mon, Lovey. We'd better go in with them." Pete obviously intended to ignore Poppy's comment, as she and Lovey left Poppy and Belle behind in the Trooper. The two older women joined Lil and her daughter and Marsha and made their way to the church.

Poppy watched them thoughtfully until they were inside. "Well," she turned to Belle, "I guess that's —" She interrupted herself to quickly raise the camera and zoom in on the occupant of a candy-apple red Porsche convertible that had just come to a sliding stop on the edge of the church lawn. "Now who th' hell do you suppose *that* is?" She watched as a tall young man raised himself by his arms and threw a muscled leg over the car door. He smoothly de-autoed and stood leaning against the little vehicle, seeming to steady himself. He was dressed in tennis sweats with a white *gimme* hat jammed on his head. He yanked it off and tossed it back into the car, revealing coppery, red curls.

"My guess is another Needham . . . but, which one?"

Belle responded, "Didn't Lovey say Marsha has a son?"

"Hmmm." Poppy followed the unsteady progress of the young man as he stopped in the shade of the awning and leaned against a support post. He ran a hand across his eyes and then pushed his fingers through his hair. He seemed to come to some inner resolution and pulled himself up tall and straight. He walked with almost poise up to the church door and leaned forward to grasp the handle. Suddenly he drew back his hand and placed it in his armpit as if to keep the hand from reaching forward again. He turned in a slow circle, a look of agony on his face. Then he slumped as if in defeat and opened the door, quickly disappearing into the darkness of the church.

"Hmmm," Poppy repeated. "Hmmm - *hmmm.* That was an interesting little dance." *Looks a lot like a fellow who doesn't jump over too many nets, hey Wondercrone?*

"Yes," Belle answered, "He *did* seem to be suffering from indecision. Not to mention a probable dose of liquid spirits."

"Yeah . . . well, I guess we'd better stow this away and sneak on in there. We don't want to make a stir."

* * * * *

38

A few moments later the two women slipped quietly through the church door and took the first empty aisle seats near the back of the church. As Poppy's eyes adjusted to the gloom, she noticed the driver of the red Porsche sitting directly in front of them. He seemed to have folded and slumped his tall slim body into a barely noticeable lump in the corner of the long wooden pew.

Poppy let her gaze travel over the people who had gathered to bid farewell to Christine Jessup. It seemed to Poppy that the larger group of mourners filled the pews to the right of the main aisle. She let her eyes focus on several individuals and made a surprising discovery. *Well - lookee here, W.C. All the lake people are over there on the left side . . . and all the river people are on our side. Seems they chose up sides for real in this part of the country.*

A movement down the aisle caught Poppy's eye. It was Lavon Gatling and she seemed to be trying to get Poppy's attention. No. Not Poppy's attention, but that of the young man who slumped, oblivious, in front of Poppy. *Wonder what Missus Sheriff Gatling wants with that young pup, Dillworth? Them's pretty big guns to be pointing at such a pitiful target.*

Lavon Gatling suddenly looked Poppy squarely in the eye and smiled, activating world-class dimples. She then turned slowly away to face the front. Even at this distance, the sensual force of the woman's gaze settled in Poppy's groin like a slug of cold maple syrup on a bite of hot, buttery waffle. She felt a shiver run down her spine, causing her to move just a little closer to Belle. *Whoooee, Dillworth. A woman needs a silver lasso and a red, white and blue suit to fight off eyes like those.*

Poppy looked away from the back of Lavon Gatling's blonde head and resumed her observation of the sacristy. It was as familiar as every Baptist church she had ever been in. A shield-shaped wooden plaque on the wall over the piano announced last week's versus this week's attendance. A poorly painted landscape rose behind the baptismal font and a semi-circle of choir chairs on risers backed up the preacher's pulpit. Today a closed white casket floated on a sea of flowers, a little to the right of where a middle-aged man waved an open Bible above his head.

"Early, early. *Too* early . . . He has taken our daughter, Naomi Christine Jessup, to His bosom."

Poppy tuned him out. Since her discovery of the Goddess, the concept of God-He was giving her a bit of trouble. She peered into the shadowy area farther to the right of the casket and discovered she could just make out the interesting fact that no one, not even one mourner, was seated in the family alcove. It was surrounded by banks of gladiola sprays, six deep in places. Poppy suspected that the florists, if there were more than one in Pecan Valley, were counting a tidy bit of change this afternoon.

Poppy noticed the four red heads of the Tyrone Needham family in the first pew on the "laker" side, flanked by groups of people whom Pete had identified as Chris' father's high-rolling friends from the larger cities around Texas. Poppy searched a couple of rows in on the "river" side and located Lovey's white head. Beside her sat Pete, whose ears glowed crimson, the hat crease dented firmly into her short, lank hair. *At least Lovey got that damn fedora off her.*

She wondered if Pete was wearing her new hearing aid. Poppy remembered her own failing hearing. One of these days she would have to face the necessity of wearing a device like Pete's. She made herself a promise. *When I do get one of these gadgets I'm gonna USE it . . . Except for preachers.*

Beside Lovey and Pete sat Marsha and Lil, their shoulders barely touching. Juno's head rested on Lil's free arm which was snuggled around her shoulders.

Poppy soon was prodded by Belle to stand to sing the hymn that Belle pointed out in the hymnal she held open in front of them.

Poppy's knees ached with a fiery insistence as she followed Belle and the others out of the church into the bright midday sunshine for the drive to the cemetery.

Less than fifteen minutes later, Poppy and Belle, along with Pete and Lovey and Juno, were standing in the shade of an oak tree which bore a plaque claiming its age to be over two hundred years. The graveside services were about to begin.

A tent-like awning of wine-red canvas had been erected over the grave-site. The casket was already in place above the opened earth. Of course no dirt was visible, dirt being deemed offensive by the people who make their living from placing dead people in it, Poppy supposed. She detected the edges of strips of artificial turf that lined the shaded area reserved for the family and close friends. And, of course, for the elderly and infirm.

Poppy leaned against the tree to lessen the stress

on her knees. She wasn't about to admit that she might be on the verge of inclusion in that last category. Since the physically taxing adventure of last Christmas at Red Rook Ranch, her knees had developed a new way of reminding her that her body was sometimes hard-pressed to carry out the requests of her brain. She longed for the walking stick that Belle had insisted she bring, but it was safe at home where her pride had left it.

Poppy let her gaze wander over the hushed crowd of people who sought shade under open umbrellas, hats, and even newspapers held over their heads. The July sun was making its presence felt. She noticed Lil and Marsha talking to a chunky man beside a van that looked like the rusted hulk of a wrecked ship. In lieu of paint, the van was plastered with decals and bumper stickers. The man's balding head shone like a dew-dappled melon as the sun reflected from droplets of perspiration across his pink forehead.

Poppy punched Lovey. "Who's that?" She nodded in the direction of the van.

"That's Melvin Mossbacker, 'Mossie' to folks 'round here. He's the star reporter for the *County Weekly*. He's no Clark Kent but he's *family*, if you know what I mean."

Poppy turned her attention back to Mossbacker, who had just opened the rear doors of the van and was pulling out equipment as Lil talked excitedly to him. Poppy was sure Lovey had meant the fellow was gay. He didn't *look* gay. He looked like a bubba. She realized with a sharp pang of chagrin that she was doing *it* again. Making judgments from appearances. Prejudice was *its* nasty name. *Yeppers, Wondercrone. You old wombat, when are you gonna learn not to do that?*

Poppy watched as Melvin Mossbacker hitched up his sagging jeans and very precisely tucked in the tails of his army-drab shirt. He then hefted a heavy-duty sports-cam to his shoulder and pointed it at Lil, obviously filming her as she spoke. He shifted it toward Marsha and captured, Poppy was sure, the searchlight of a smile that served as punctuation for whatever Marsha was telling him.

The two women evidently concluded their remarks and Lil motioned toward the cemetery, as if to indicate that Mossbacker should capture the scene with his camera. By this time Mossbacker's shirttail had pulled free and ridden up to expose an unappealing expanse of hairy middle. Poppy watched, fascinated as the dark seductive eye on his navel winked open and shut as he moved to film the rest of the crowd. The spell was broken as two men in dark suits and darker glasses appeared on either side of Mossbacker and quietly hustled him back to the rear of the van. He lowered his yellow camera and glared.

One of the men took the camera from him and smoothly ejected the tape, then slipped it into an inside jacket pocket. The sun glinted from something metallic under the man's suit coat. As Mossbacker watched, the two men quickly slipped back into the throng of mourners milling about the grounds.

Well well, W.C. Just who do those toughies work for? The "lakers" or the "rivers?" And why should either side care if Mossie films the funeral?

Poppy's inner musings were interrupted as Lil and Marsha approached, both apparently unaware of Mossbacker's troubles.

"Hey, Lil. Your friend's tape just got hijacked by a couple of slickers."

The women turned to look, just in time to see the van pulling away from the curb. Evidently Mossbacker had taken the warning to heart.

"You see who it was, Poppy?"

"Yeah. Two guys. Looked like a couple of bit-players from *Mission Impossible*."

"Shit," Lil muttered.

Marsha's usually composed expression clouded and a little muscle worked in her jaw as she watched the van round the corner and go out of sight.

Poppy added, "They didn't dress like locals, if that's a help. Real snappy dark suits and wraparound sunshades."

"Oh, crap," Lil said, her shoulders drooping. "It sounds like the Bosco brothers."

"Well, evidently they didn't know who they were messing with." Poppy chuckled and nudged Lil's shoulder. "Look up there." She nodded up toward the roof of a low cement-block garage across the street where Melvin Mossbacker was scuttling forward along the roof ledge with his camera already to his shoulder.

The services were soon over and the women all returned to Hallelujah Bend, except for Lil and Marsha who left for Dallas to deliver a load of Lil's goddess sculptures to a gallery. The hot day had sapped Poppy's energy and she longed for a cool nap. She wanted to be fresh for tomorrow's planned fishing expedition to the catfish ponds. She couldn't really do much yet about solving the mystery except maybe a trip tomorrow morning to look around at the Jessup place.

CHAPTER THREE
A Game of Cat and Mouse

After lunch with Pete and Juno and Lovey, Poppy and Belle retired to their cabin and stripped to tee-shirts and panties to get some relief from the heat. They tried to rest on the sturdy double bed in the *Lorena Hickok*, the largest and most comfortable of Hallelujah Bend's cabins. It was the only cabin besides the *Colette* that boasted an air conditioner. The ceiling fan spun a wobbly spell over them, doing

47

its best to circulate the refrigerated air wheezing from the window unit.

"Whoooeee." Poppy mopped her forehead with a damp bandanna. "I forgot how hot it can get down here. A little bitty old rain shower wouldn't hurt a thing. Settle some of this dust, too."

"Mmm-hmm," Belle answered. She leaned on her elbow and looked down at Poppy. "Is it too hot for snuggling?"

Poppy grinned. "Nope." She pulled Belle to her. "Got to have my daily snuggles. Don't want to get into a snuggle deficit situation."

Belle nestled her head against Poppy's shoulder for a moment, then raised up again. "Papillon, what do you make of those two thugs who accosted that Mossbacker fellow? It's too bad Lil and Marsha had to go to Dallas after the funeral . . . and I wish Lovey'd been able to reach Mossbacker. Don't you think he could help us sort out some of this?"

"I really don't know, honey. It's too early yet to tell who all the teams are, much less the players. And something's bothering me . . ." Poppy turned on her side to face Belle. She breathed in the pleasant smell of her hair and the powdery hint of talcum. She pressed her lips to Belle's cheek, savoring the softness. "You know something else?" she murmured, her lips still grazing Belle's satiny skin.

Belle laughed and pulled away. "Now which is it going to be? Sweet nothings or Sherlock stuff?"

Poppy smiled up at Belle, her heart full with happiness. "I guess we might's well mull over what took place today. It's too damn hot for where sweet nothings might lead us."

Belle nodded and dabbed at her temples with the

hem of her tee-shirt. Poppy's hand crept toward the creamy mound of breast exposed by Belle's temple-dabbing motion. She caught her breath sharply as the sight provoked an insistent pulsing between her legs. "Mercy, Belle. How can I concentrate if you keep flashing me like that?"

Belle primly snapped her shirttail down and moved a few inches away on the bed. "All right now, Papillon. You were saying that something else about today is bothering you?"

"Yeah." Poppy sobered at the reminder. "It seemed to me there wasn't a lot of real grieving going on today. I mean, I didn't see anyone just exactly prostrate over Chris Jessup's death. Except Marsha's son, who came up at the last there at the church."

"Hmm." Belle mused. "Come to think of it, it does seem odd. Of course there was no family there since the poor young woman had no kin." She tilted her chin at Poppy. "There sure seemed to be a coolness between Marsha and the boy, too. Lovey said his name is Tom Ross. Wonder what caused the problem between him and his mother? I noticed he wasn't at the cemetery, either."

A tiny click sounded in Poppy's brain. *Wonder who gets all the Jessup land and money?* She needed to make a list of questions soon. She turned her attention back to Belle who was still speaking.

"But, you'd think there'd have been some of Chris's friends there, wouldn't you? We don't really know much about Christine Jessup, do we, dear?"

"Nopers," Poppy answered. "Not near enough. I think we should start our investigation bright and early tomorrow, don't you?"

49

Poppy rolled over and grabbed the phone. She dialed rapidly. "Hello, Pete?" She raised her voice, shouting into the mouthpiece. "Put your *hearing aid* on!" She paused, listening for a moment, then shouted again. "*Hey, Pete!*" She grinned suddenly and lowered her voice. "Oh. Hi Lovey. Say, can you do something for us? . . . Well, it's something only you can do, I think. We need to take a look at the Jessup place. Didn't you say you still have the key Chris gave you? . . . Okay. Breakfast? Yeah. Sounds good. When? Okay, we'll see you 'bout six a.m."

Poppy replaced the phone and grinned as Belle fell backward on the bed in a mock swoon. "Yeah. I know that's pretty early. We've slipped into some bad habits, haven't we? These country women get up *early.*"

The next morning, Sunday, July second, Poppy and Belle ate breakfast with Lovey and Pete and Juno in the kitchen of the lavender farmhouse. The "purple palace," Poppy had dubbed it. Pete and Juno, with Kali tagging behind, left to tend the catfish ponds. The other three women quickly washed and put away the dishes and boarded the Trooper for the trip to the Springs.

It was ten minutes before eight when they turned off the road and passed through the main gates of the Jessup place. Tall, mortared limestone pillars stood on either side of the drive, connected at the top by a curving, wrought iron arch. In the center of the arch, above a banner announcing *The Springs,* an open book was depicted in rusty iron.

The Bible, Poppy thought, recognizing its familiar background of the three crosses of Christianity.

The road wound through a pecan orchard where the trees had all been whitewashed to about six feet up the trunks. Lovey had evidently earned her pay from the Jessups. The orchards were neat and well-tended. Though the morning sunshine slanted in brightly between the trees, there was no dew to reflect its light. The grass in the orchard was neatly mowed, but it stood sparse and spiky in the dry ground, like a punk haircut.

"Now watch out up here a little piece, Poppy. The road narrows a bit where we cross that wooden bridge yonder over the spring branch. It's too bad the springs aren't flowing anymore. They dried up four years ago when the Woodards on the next farm over deepened their irrigation wells. That's the driver behind the idea to dam up the river. All those wells have depleted the underground aquifer and the farmers are clamoring for surface water."

Poppy paid close attention to Lovey's warning as they crossed the low bridge and left the flat bottom land of the pecan orchard behind. They entered a dense woods of juniper and oak where the road curved and climbed steeply through deep cuts into the limestone strata. She mused about the proposed lake and the problems and the solutions it presented.

"*Godamighty!*" Poppy shouted and swung the Trooper hard to the right to avoid hitting a low red sports car that shot past them and quickly disappeared down the hill. Poppy stopped the vehicle and sat still, grasping the steering wheel, trying to calm her pounding heart.

"Jesusmaryandjoseph. Where did that fool come from?"

Lovey answered, "That was Tom Ross Needham. Marsha's boy. And I'd say he came from where we're headed. Up at the Jessup's place. This here's the private drive to the Springs. No place else he *could've* been."

Belle said, "Poppy . . . That was —"

"Yeah, I know," Poppy interrupted. "The young fellow from the church. He seems to be the only one in the county showing any emotion about the whole affair . . . and I'd say *he's* verging on *manic.*"

The thumping in Poppy's heart had slowed. She looked in both mirrors and carefully pulled back onto the road.

"Now, why do you suppose he was here, Lovey?" Poppy asked. She gazed at her friend's face in the rearview mirror.

Lovey's jaw went slack for a half-second and her eyelids flickered behind the large lenses of her glasses. "Uh . . . well. Your guess is as good as mine. How should I know?"

Poppy said, "Well, Lovey. Be sensible, girl. You've been living here all your life. Of course my guess is *not* as good as yours. Have you ever seen him here before? Does he have some connection with the Jessups?"

Again Poppy caught the quiver to Lovey's jaw as Lovey answered. "I can't keep up with every young buck in the county. Besides, Tom and Marsha have kind of been on the outs about her taking up with Lil. One thing you learn when you live in community, Poppy — you don't go around tending to

52

other folks' business. If you want to know anything about Tom Ross, you oughta ask Marsha." Lovey sucked her lips against her teeth and turned her head away, clearly finished with the subject.

"Oh . . . Okay, Lovey. You're right. I didn't think about the propriety of the whole thing. I'll take it up with Marsha, later."

Things seemed to be happening a little faster than Poppy had expected. The sensation she called "the feeling" began to creep up the nape of her neck. That old feeling of excited anticipation mixed with hole-in-the-stomach dread. That same feeling of confident exhilaration she had felt ever since her first deer hunt as a girl of ten, when she had found her quarry, brought it down, field-dressed it and hauled it home to her grateful mother.

They had made it through a hard Depression winter on the strength of that hunt and in Poppy's mind it had been the fulcrum upon which balanced the two parts of her youth. That of the helpless, dependent girlchild and that of the young warrior-woman who would take that same "feeling" into every future fray, excited with success and the sure belief that she could win if only she tried hard enough.

Of course, we didn't count on the good ole patriarchy, did we, Fearless Tracker? All those years in between then and now. Gone all to hell in a handcart.

Poppy maneuvered the Trooper back onto the road and they covered the remaining distance to the Springs without incident. Soon a large white farmhouse rose into view, nestled on the green hill like a fat mother hen, its extended wings spread over the grass as if to shelter the people who lived there.

"Odd-looking house," Poppy commented. "With all those porches spread out like that."

"Yeah," Lovey answered. "It is a bit odd-looking, but it'd make a wonderful Cronesnest." She looked wistfully at the old house. "But, there's not enough money in the building fund to even *begin* to make a down payment." She turned her attention back to Poppy. "See, all the folks in the church helped the Jessups build the main part of that house in eighteen eighty-eight. When Mama was a girl she used to work for old Nathan Jessup, who came to Hermosa county as a single man after the Civil War. Funny thing about the Jessups. Each one of 'em had only one child, a son, until Christine came along. Mama told me lots of tales about the Springs . . . but, then my mama was a good one for tales. She could crank one out about just anybody you'd name. I never put much stock in 'em, though. Mama tended a little toward puffery."

"Well, Lovey," Poppy said, "I believe that's one of the longest speeches I ever heard you make." She winked at Belle. "If I've got it straight, you're telling me there aren't any other Jessups around. Guess Chris was the last one, huh?"

"Well. That's all the ones anybody 'round here ever heard of, anyhow."

Poppy let the vehicle roll to a stop beside a sagging picket fence. Two large calico cats leaped from the front porch steps and hurried toward Lovey as she got out. They began to dance in leaning figure eights around and between her ankles. In a surprisingly agile manner, Lovey bent and picked them up and turned to Poppy. "This is Sibyl and Sophie. I been coming over every day and feeding them. They belonged to Chris. Don't know what'll become of them now. I'd like to have them, but you know how Pete is about cats. Won't have one on the place."

Poppy glanced at Belle, who she was sure had just mentally demoted Pete to the rank of cretin, or below.

"Humph," Belle sniffed, and ran her hand lightly across the chest of the nearest cat. "Maybe Cleo would like to have some company."

Jesusmaryandjoseph and all the suffering angels. Cleo is enough cat for TEN lesbians. No, Belle. Get ahold, girl. We don't need any more cats! What we need is a big old hairy, comes-when-you-call-her DOG!

"Harumph." Poppy cleared her throat and tried to redirect traffic. "Is it all right if we come in, Lovey?"

"Yeah." She lowered the cats to the ground. They scurried quickly away and disappeared into the house. Poppy and Belle followed Lovey up the steps of a screened-in porch which ran the whole length of the house. Poppy noticed the paint was flaking badly and the roof gutters had come loose in places and leaned away from their moorings. Unlike the well-tended orchards, this place had an air of general neglect. Many more months without maintenance and it would advance into a state of obvious disrepair.

"I'll feed those two while you take your peek around." Lovey motioned them to go.

Poppy stopped her with, "How hard would it be for us to have a look at Chris's room?"

"Oh. Well, I think that would be okay." Lovey nodded toward a doorway. "Chris always used the old section of the house when she was here."

Belle asked, "Was she here often?"

"No. Not really . . . She was away at one school or another for most of her growing up years. This past year is the longest time she's been here since she was a child. She had just got her degree in sociology or somesuch out in California last year, when her folks were killed in that plane crash up in Oklahoma."

"She have any close friends, Lovey?" Poppy asked, turning to look evenly at her old friend.

"Chris was mostly a loner." Lovey set her jaw and pursed her lips in a manner which indicated she was anxious to settle the mewing cats.

"Okay," Poppy said. "Just two more quickies. Did anyone from the law come out here when Chris died?"

"The Sheriff and Tyrone Needham from the bank came to close up the place. Since I already had a key to come in and take care of the livestock, they came by the camp and asked if I'd continue to do it until the estate was settled. I don't know if anyone else came out here or not."

"Hmmm," Poppy mused, looking down at the tops of her hands for a second. "What about fellas?" Poppy looked back up at Lovey. "Did Chris have any suitors?"

Lovey's eyelids flickered. She blinked rapidly as she disengaged from Poppy's gaze and half-turned impatiently. "Can't, uh, say for sure about that."

Poppy felt Belle's hand on her arm. She turned to look at her. "Yeah, you're right, hon. Thanks, Lovey. We'll holler when we're through, okay?"

Lovey nodded and hurried away.

Poppy squared her shoulders and said, "Well, let's take a look at that unfortunate young woman's room."

They followed Lovey's directions and easily found their way through the old house. The door to Chris Jessup's room was closed, but moved open at Poppy's touch. At first glance the room seemed orderly, but after a few seconds of observation, Poppy realized something was wrong.

Squared up stacks of flyers took up most of the space on top of a low cedar chest, but the stacks were all skewed just a bit, as if someone had lifted the lid without first removing the flyers.

A large, old-fashioned oak dresser stood between two tall windows. Its drawers were all closed but the top one appeared to be pushed in about a half-inch too far, its face sunk back from the next one down.

Poppy stood just inside the room with Belle close behind her. She let her mind register the room's contents, cataloguing pertinent details with the part of her brain which had, for forty years with the Caliche County Sheriff's Department, given her a reputation for almost total recall. Of course, aging had dulled the edges somewhat, but, she thought, *but* thank the Goddess for modern technology and the video camera. *Yeah, Wondercrone. The same video camera you left in the cabin? Smooth move.*

Poppy spoke aloud, in response to her inner voice. "Well. Old blue-eyes'll just have to wing it this time." She turned to Belle. "Let's take a peek in and around and under."

On the wall above a cluttered desk hung a colored map of the proposed lake. Poppy moved closer and leaned forward squinting, to get a better look at the markings someone had added to it. She jerked her offending spectacles from her face and rubbed at the lenses. Plopping them once more on her nose she peered closely at the map. Someone, she thought, probably Christine Jessup, had marked several areas along the river course with either X's or O's. Probably to indicate who was for and who was against the dam. *Cat and mouse, W.C.?*

Poppy moved on to examine the contents of the desk drawer. She had just pulled it out when Belle exclaimed, "Look here, Papillon." Belle pointed to the dresser drawer she herself had pulled out. "I think someone's been rooting around in here. Things are still folded, but they're kind of jumbled around."

Poppy looked in at the layers of underwear. "Yeppers — in fact, this whole room looks as if someone's been searching for something. They were pretty careful, but you can tell they were in a hurry or something." She pointed back to the desk. "Whoever it was must've found what they were looking for before they got to the desk. Everything in there looks pretty orderly."

"Yes," Belle mused. "Or they got scared off before they found what they were after."

Belle stepped to the window nearest the bed. "This window's not quite shut either. See?" She lifted the sash easily, opening the window wide as Poppy bent forward for a closer look.

"Um-hmmm," Poppy answered and poked her

finger toward the windowscreen latch-hook. "Screen's unhooked, too. Seems too much of a coincidence to me. Wonder if this is the work of that young fellow in the red car?" She pushed her finger against the frame of the windowscreen. It swung outward at the bottom. Poppy leaned in closer until the top of her head was against the screen. She peered down at the ground beneath the window.

"Whoa!" She jumped back. The dark space outside the window turned white and orange and black as Chris Jessup's orphaned cats leaped from the top of a wooden box into the room. "Hey! Easy there, girls . . ." The friendly, just-fed cats wound themselves around Poppy's ankles meowing as they followed each other in a neat double helix. "Belle?" Poppy looked beseechingly at her partner.

Belle smiled and picked up the cats. She sat on the bed petting them while Poppy regained her poise.

"Damn," Poppy said as she patted the area over her racing heart. "Those varmints nearly gave me the big one. Toss them back out there, Belle, and let's get Lovey back to the camp and get our fish-poles out. Pete and Juno'll have all the big ones caught if we don't watch out. And my heart's had enough jolts for today. Maybe the visit tomorrow with Sheriff Gatling won't produce any startling surprises."

Poppy watched as Belle wordlessly held out the screen and let the two calicos out through the opening. She turned to face Poppy with a mischievous smile dancing at the corners of her mouth. "Nothing more startling than the Sheriff's wife . . . perhaps?"

Poppy felt her ears start to glow as a blush rose up her upper body. *Uh-oh, W.C. Caught redhanded in hooterville.* Lamely she said, "Heh, heh, heh. Well, you'll be there to protect me, won'tcha?"

The afternoon fishing expedition had gone well and the smell of frying catfish made Poppy's mouth water. Pete had also set a few fillets to broil over mesquite coals and Lovey had produced home-made hushpuppies. Quart jars of iced tea sat on a wooden side table making wet rings on the dry surface.

The day was still hot, but the sun had dipped below the line of treetops across the valley. The only wind stirring came from an ancient box fan Pete had placed on the porch steps. Despite the perspiration trickling down her neck, Poppy wondered if she'd ever been happier. To be with her lover and good friends and eat fish she had caught herself and scratch the head of a big friendly dog . . . what more could an old dyke possibly want?

Kali startled Poppy by standing suddenly and *woofing* in the direction of the driveway. *Well, that's either Mossbacker's van or the Wreck of the Hesperus on wheels.* Poppy's stomach tightened with irritation as two men got out and walked through the gate and into her perfect evening. Kali danced shamelessly for Mossbacker and his companion. *Humph. That dog's certainly liberal with her affections.* Poppy made the corners of her mouth lift into what she hoped was a pleasant expression as Lil introduced the two men and Belle and invited them to supper.

Mossbacker grinned, filling his plate, and waved a wide hand in the direction of the tall thin young man who was throwing a Frisbee with Juno and Kali. "*I* don't mind if I do, but Ralph only eats nuts and grains and things I can't pronounce." He looked at his lover, his eyes soft with admiration. "But, isn't he gorgeous, though?"

Poppy thought he *was* a fine looking fellow. A little poetic maybe, with dark hollows beneath his eyes and a prominent Prince Charles nose, but still interesting to look at.

Melvin Mossbacker sat on the porch step by Poppy's chair, expertly balancing a plate of fish on his knee while he washed down hush-puppies with great swallows of iced tea. "Lil tells me you saw the Bosco brothers purloin my tape at the funeral."

"Yeah, I did." Poppy, watching the young man mop creamy slaw juice from his plate with a fried corn-doggie, remembered fondly the days when she could eat like that, the days before her gallbladder had gone gravelly. "What's with those guys, anyhow? They sure were out of line."

Mossbacker frowned. "That's not the first time I've had trouble with those two. Word is, they've staked everything they have, or ever *hope* to have, on the lake coming in. They've always been into some seedy business or other here in the county, but nothing as big as what they hope to do with their Bosco Bluffs Marina and Condo Club." Mossbacker's eyes widened and he set his plate aside as he warmed to what was evidently a subject dear to him. "If fools like the Boscos and other ranchers hadn't let their cattle over-graze and hadn't planted on the watersheds, we wouldn't be facing this mess now. The rainwater can't soak in any more. The topsoil runs off and —" He looked up as Ralph joined them. "Oh, hi, honey."

Ralph smiled at his impassioned lover and placed a long-fingered hand on his shoulder. "I heard you revving up your engines for your favorite speech." He looked down at Melvin with obvious affection. "I just wanted to remind you we still have to go to Dallas tonight and pick up a load of flyers." He turned to Poppy. "Maybe you could ask questions and we'll try to answer them."

Poppy nodded warmly at the deep-voiced young man, her initial irritation having now been replaced with a growing admiration. "You're right. I do have a few questions. Like why didn't the Bosco brothers want you to film the funeral?"

Melvin answered. "Because they knew I would use it to stir up sympathy for the *Save the River* group. Which I *am* doing, thank you very much."

Poppy asked, "Where is the Boscos' home base? How can I get a chance to talk to them?"

"Ned and Ted have a butane-propane gas business over on Highway Sixty-Seven, but the best time to get a look at those two doin' their slimy doin's would be at the July the Fourth thing at the park in Pecan Valley, day after tomorrow."

Ralph nodded his agreement and added, "They're going to have a booth set up and they're raffling off a ski-boat after the parade. One of their good buddies, Sheriff Troy Gatling, is gonna be giving lessons on how to bass-fish . . . If you can stand the smell, you might even catch all three of 'em at once."

Poppy could hardly wait. Nothing pleased her more than working subtle revenge on "suck-egg" sheriffs and their good buddies.

CHAPTER FOUR
Games and Players

The next morning Poppy and Belle parked the Trooper beside a row of pecan trees along the Pecan Valley courthouse lawn. A metal sign shaped like a broken arrow indicated they would find the Sheriff's office inside and downstairs.

They entered the building and headed for the brass stair rail. Halfway down the worn marble steps, Poppy realized someone was flagrantly disobeying the No Smoking order. Stale cigar smoke wafted past them on poor air-conditioning. The stairwell was barely cooler than the outside temperature. Even at this early hour the day bore promise of a three-digit afternoon.

Poppy, with Belle close behind, pushed open a wooden door upon which was painted a five-pointed gold star. She braced herself against the feelings that grabbed her stomach and throat at the same time. The anguish that always accompanied memories of her forty years as a clerk for the Caliche County Sheriff's Department now threatened to overcome her. As a private investigator with a recently solved murder case to her credit, she knew she *should* feel confident, but —

Suck it up, girl. Get a grip. That was then and this is now, Dillworth. We got a job to do here and — Poppy's inner dialogue came to an abrupt halt as she was jostled backward by the hip-pocket side of a tall man in a tan uniform who appeared suddenly, his back to the women.

"Hey," the startled lawbreaker said around the wet end of a large cigar, as he turned to face Poppy. "Hey," he said again in a different tone. His hand fell away from the butt of his pistol and he appeared to inspect first Poppy and then Belle from behind his Ray-Bans as if they stood in a line-up. He stuck his jaw out at Poppy, still mouthing his words around the cigar. "I'm Sheriff Gatling. What can I do for you little ladies?"

Poppy wondered briefly if there was a laboratory somewhere in the South that cloned these men and issued them all standard dark aviator glasses. No wonder the stereotype found its way into so many movies. It was based on the reality of the condescending male chauvinist who now took her proffered hand in both of his and *patted* it.

Poppy shucked her chagrin along with the failed handshake and answered. "Name's P.A. Dillworth. This here's my partner, Belle Stoner. We're private investigators. Like to ask you a few questions about the death of Christine Jessup." She flashed her I.D. and P.I. license at him and was happy to watch his mouth settle into a grim line as he read it.

The Sheriff removed his glasses and closed them with a neat one-handed flip just before they slid into his shirt pocket. Without the glasses, his face had the raccoon tan of someone who spent a lot of time in the sun. He moved backward into the office, motioning with his chin for the women to follow him.

"Accidental drowning. No witnesses. The case is closed," he responded tersely. "Not much to investigate." He remained standing and pointedly did not offer a seat to the two women. Chauvinism did have its up side, Poppy supposed, when it came to offering elderly women a chair, but all in all she guessed she'd rather have stiff knees and equal treatment.

"Who you working for?" He looked at Poppy suspiciously.

"Lil Turnbow."

The Sheriff's eyes narrowed and his Adam's apple worked as he retrieved his sunglasses. "I'm sorry. I can't give you any more information. But like I said, it was an accident . . . now if you'll excuse me, I was just on my way out when you ladies came in."

He moved meaningfully to the door and held it open. To the Sheriff, at least, the conversation was clearly over.

Poppy turned toward the door with an efficient about-face, saying, "Oh, that's all right. We'll be here till we solve the case." She waited for Belle to clear the doorway, then followed her into the hall.

Belle asked, "When's the next town meeting, Sheriff Gatling?" She continued speaking as they started up the stairway. "From what we've been able to gather so far, there'll probably be a bunch of folks there who might've had a pretty good motive for getting Christine Jessup out of their hair."

Sheriff Troy Gatling stopped in mid-climb, with one foot two stairs above the other. He slowly removed the cigar from his mouth and leaned toward the two women. "You need to watch out now, who you go stirring up. There's already too much bad blood in Pecan Valley . . . you're liable to end up breaking a hip or something." He jammed his hat on his head and pushed his way past them and up the stairs.

Belle sputtered and stopped her climb as he disappeared from sight. "Break a *hip*? Why that puffed-up piss-ant. Was that a threat, Papillon? What do you think he was trying to say?"

Poppy leaned against the rail for a moment before she answered. "I think he was trying to tell us to mind our own business. But, the town meeting *is* our business. If we want to find out what really happened to Chris Jessup, that is."

They continued up the stairs as Poppy wondered what, aside from the usual homophobic reaction, was behind the Sheriff's apparent distaste for Lil

Turnbow. Did he know about his wife's afternoon in Lil's studio at the camp? Most men Poppy had known did not take kindly to playing cuckold. *'Specially if the other man was a woman, huh, Wondercrone?*

Poppy's inner musing took a quick second place to the sight which greeted them as they pushed through the courthouse outer door. Sheriff Troy Gatling, hat in hand, sans cigar, was backed against a tree trunk by the long lacquered nail on his wife's right index finger. Lavon "Gunner" Gatling apparently saw Poppy and Belle, because her demeanor changed immediately from intimidating to friendly and open.

"See *you* later." She patted her husband's chest in dismissal and walked toward the two women.

Boomchicka-boom. Poppy's inner ear supplied the sound track for the woman's performance. Lavon Gatling was wearing a black Spandex one-piece workout suit with a neckline that plunged to the waist, below which a hint of shadowy hipbone peeked from cut-outs on both sides. Her surprisingly muscular thighs were bare but her shoes were serious-looking Rykas with purposeful straps and ties. Hot pink leg warmers rose over shapely calves. The leprechaun in Poppy's heart rapped a shillelagh against her ribs.

"Hel-*lo*. I'm Lavon Gatling." She extended her hands, one to Belle and one to Poppy. "Troy tells me you are private investigators. How ex*cit*ing."

Lavon Gatling's voice matched the rest of her. Seductive, but with a definite purpose. Like the soft touch of the nurse's cotton swab before the needle's prick. And with a lilting tendency to drop for emphasis on certain syllables. Syllables also emphasized by long lashes which lowered over eyes of dusky onyx.

Belle responded, "Yes, it is. Exciting. Sometimes more than others." She glanced at Poppy. "I'm Belle Stoner. This is my *silent* partner, Papillon Dillworth."

Poppy hated it when anyone used her real name. She preferred to use her initials or even her nickname. But in this instance, she guessed she deserved Belle's little jab. She *had* been struck dumb by the twin mounds of creamy flesh which formed an inviting valley beneath Lavon Gatling's collarbones. *Yeppers. Hooterville. No wonder Lovey accused Pete of wanting to put her nose in there. Whoooee.*

"Harumph." *Keep this up, W.C. and you'll be sleeping on the porch with Kali.* "Pleased to meetcha." Poppy struggled to regain a little poise. At sixty-five a lesbian was supposed to be wise and above all that. *Hmmm . . . above all that? What a picture, W.C.* Poppy had the cold-syrup-hot-waffle feeling again in the entire lower half of her body. Except for the toes on her left foot, where Belle had deftly placed the heel of her Rockport Walker and was insistently pressing down with all of her one hundred and nine pounds. Poppy suddenly remembered why she was in Pecan Valley and said, "If you have a few minutes, Miz Gatling, we'd like to ask you some questions."

"Please call me Gunner." Long lashes lowered. "Everyone else does." Lashes came up allowing Poppy a glimpse into smoky depths. "Actually, I'm just on my way to aerobics class." Lavon Gatling's thumbs slid under the hip holes in the stretchy fabric of her workout suit, lifting it away from her skin. Like a little girl holding a dress hem, she curtsied, then let the Spandex snap back into place. "But," she said, "maybe you could drop by my house at two o'clock this afternoon?" She retrieved a business card from her workout bag and handed it to Poppy.

"Uh, sure." Poppy took the card and slipped it into her hip pocket without looking at it. "We can do that."

"Bye for now, then." Lavon Gatling trotted toward a white Jeep Laredo that seemed to be equipped with everything a person would need if she were going on safari. Several antennas whipped the air as the four-wheel-drive vehicle moved off down the street on its oversized knobby tires.

Belle pointedly pinched Poppy's rear as she fished Gunner Gatling's card from Poppy's pocket. "Well, Papillon, you certainly added a new meaning to the word *ogle*."

"Now, hon," Poppy began, but stopped short when she saw the crease between Belle's brows.

"You did. You ogled."

Poppy looked down at the tops of her hands and inspected her nails. Sometimes it was best to just admit character flaws and get on with life. "Yeah. You're right. I did." She raised her eyes and grinned what she hoped was her best blue-eyed grin. "Tried not to. Couldn't help it. The woman ought to have those things registered."

Belle relented with a sigh. "They *are* nice, aren't they?"

Okay, W.C. We know that question needs no spoken answer.

71

Aloud Poppy asked, "What's the card say?" She took it from Belle's extended fingers and turned it to the light. It said simply, *Lavon Gatling — Real Estate*, and gave an address and phone number. She slipped it back into her pocket. "How's about we go across the street to the bank over there and see if we can get a few minutes with Tyrone Needham. I'd like to get an idea of just exactly how much this lake business means to the commercial establishment here in Pecan Valley."

Poppy looked over at Belle as they stepped from the shade out into the sunlight. Belle's profile was majestic. Poppy wanted to run her hand over the sparkling aura of white hair that had come loose from Belle's thick braid. She wanted to hold her and kiss her on the place where her turquoise and silver earrings moved against her neck as she walked. Poppy shocked herself by leaning close and whispering, "You sure look beautiful today."

A crimson spot appeared on Belle's neck and spread into an appealing blush. As they entered the welcome cool of the bank lobby, Belle turned to Poppy, a look of pleased surprise still on her face. She gazed deeply into Poppy's eyes. "You look pretty good yourself, you know."

Poppy felt a matching blush heat her own face. *Get a grip, Wondercrone. The banker'll think we've got something catching if we go in there all fevered up.*

"Well, lookee here," Poppy exclaimed as she caught sight of a large diorama, grateful for a reason to change the course of their conversation. She and Belle stood near the table-high depiction of the proposed lake. The model was attractive and

72

well made. Someone, Poppy thought, had gone to great expense to display the touted merits of the dam and subsequent lake. Charts and graphs covered the wall above the table, all of them slanted toward the growth and cash flow soon to be experienced by all residents of Hermosa County. One poster proclaimed *Share the River. A Dam Will Spread It Out. Vote for Progress.*

Belle said softly, "No doubt where the bank stands on the issue."

"Nopers." Poppy tried to visualize where the original path of the river was. That piece of information was pointedly not visible. The lake was painted a brilliant blue with a tiny orange marina labelled *Bosco Bluffs* along its northern shore. One could only imagine the drowned land and houses beneath the lake's blue surface. "No doubt at all where the *bank* stands. Let's go see Mr. Tyrone Needham." She nodded toward the information desk where a young woman with a balloon of shoulder-wide hair was looking brightly in their direction.

Poppy walked toward the desk. She asked to see Mr. Needham and was asked to wait. Poppy experienced an insight as the shapely young woman walked away. *The girl had to be hired for her hair, W.C.* The pretty faces around the lobby were almost interchangeable, but hair like that, she decided, must only come once in a bank's lifetime.

Poppy had just turned to indicate to Belle where they should sit when the tall, red-haired figure of the bank president appeared at her elbow. "Good morning ladies. I'm Tyrone Needham. What may we do for you today?" He appeared to have his eyebrows permanently raised in an expectant expression. Always hopeful, Poppy supposed, that every new face was a probable depositor.

Poppy stuck out her hand. "Name's P.A. Dillworth. Me'n my partner, Belle Stoner, would like to ask you a few questions. Maybe we could go someplace where it's a little more private."

The banker's face glowed even more as he appeared to smell sums of money so large they could only be discussed away from the ears of lesser employees of the Pecan Valley State Bank. He led them down a corridor of the old building and into a walnut panelled room appointed by someone with a great love of luxury. He indicated two dark leather chairs which gleamed with the heads of brass nails where the glossy wood arms and legs were joined. "Please have a seat." He adjusted the light and caressed the leaf of a large potted palm as he sat personably on the edge of a wide leather-topped desk. He leaned toward them and rubbed his hands together sensuously, like a woman applying hand cream. "Now, how may our bank be of service?"

Poppy figured to set him straight right away. "We're not here to make a deposit, Mr. Needham. Actually, we're here to get some information about the proposed lake."

Tyrone Needham's eyes gleamed as he went off on another mental path paved with imaginary dollars. "The bank has some prime properties for sale if you ladies are interested in real estate."

Poppy tried again. "No, we're not land speculators either. We're private investigators working on the Jessup case. We understand the Jessup estate is being handled through your bank."

74

The relaxed man who had leaned toward them from his seat on the corner of the desk appeared to close like a morning glory at sunset. He drew away from Poppy and stood beside his desk, still smiling but with his eyebrows at half-mast. "Oh. Well," he said, sounding a little like Jack Benny. "Well . . . I'm afraid anything connected with the Jessup estate would have to be handled through an attorney." He closed his mouth tightly and appeared to be trying to find some way to end the conversation.

Poppy seized he moment. "Musta been a pretty big chunk of cash and real estate left when Emory Jessup and his wife were killed in that plane crash last year."

Tyrone Needham walked behind the desk and stuffed his hands into his trouser pockets. The phone rang and he excused himself to answer it, a fretful look about his mouth. "Yes . . . yes, Glo, I did. No, I won't forget." The fretful look turned into one of embarrassment. "Tell the girls not to worry, I've *already* mailed a check for next year's dorm fees . . . I'm *busy*, Gloria . . . yes. Goodbye."

Poppy intercepted a look from Belle which seemed to ask if Poppy thought what *she* must be thinking about the banker and his wife. Poppy sent her one back that said she did. Poppy looked at Tyrone Needham and asked with sudden sobriety, "Did you know Christine Jessup?"

Needham sat down, folding his lanky body carefully into his chair as his fingertips met in measured precision. "Yes. I knew her. But only as a depositor in the bank. She was here occasionally to sign various documents as necessary to the business of her parents' estate." He leaned forward and,

Poppy thought, deftly changed the subject. "You say you two ladies are private investigators? There *have* been rumors about Christine's death. But, these days it seems as if everyone in Hermosa County has had some grief come into their lives because of the lake-river controversy."

He rose and went to the window, dramatic in profile, appearing to be caught up in thoughts of his own private grievances. He turned suddenly, as if just remembering his guests. "I do hope you find it was only a tragic accident. Pecan Valley doesn't need any more strife just now." He walked toward the door and held it open in what had to be an invitation for Poppy and Belle to exit.

Seems like we're getting the bum's rush all over town, doesn't it, Wondercrone? Poppy rose, saying, "Thank you, Mr. Needham. I'll have my attorney contact the bank's attorney with my list of questions." She thought she saw the banker pale, but she couldn't be sure. Despite the panelled room's opulence, it was poorly lighted. "Thanks for your time."

When they were back out on the street in front of the bank Poppy asked, "Why don't we go in here and sit for a while?" She turned toward the inviting doorway of *The Nut House Cafeteria*. Belle followed her inside. Poppy looked around the room and spied an empty corner table. "Let's get some lunch and make some notes on what we've learned so far."

An hour and a half and four cups of decaf and two excellent chef salads later, Poppy and Belle drove toward the address on Lavon Gatling's card. The street they now travelled was the only avenue in Pecan Valley, and wound around and up a hill. The houses were old but well kept by owners who obviously had money. The wide sloping lawns settled neatly in the shade of pecan and walnut trees older than the town itself.

Belle turned to Poppy. "You don't suppose *that's* it, do you?" She pointed toward a stone and brick mansion that commanded the entire crest of the hill. White columns stood in front of long, deep verandas which ran the whole length of the two-story building.

"Yeppers. I s'pose it is. The number's right." Poppy turned the blue Isuzu into a circular drive and parked in the shade by an inviting portico which led to a massive front door. "Wow. Looks like the Gatlings take their real estate real serious. I'd sure like to know the story behind this place . . . I mean, Sheriffs are *always* underpaid. Unless this is old family property, it must be supported by Gunner's real estate business."

As they stepped along the shaded walk, Belle stopped to inspect the flowerbeds where banks and boxes of pink petunias and periwinkles grew in ordered profusion. "Well," she pronounced, "these flowers didn't get this way by accident." She waved a hand toward the rest of the yard. "These are the results of a full-time gardener."

Poppy pushed the buzzer and waited for the pleasant sound of chimes to bring someone to open the heavy door. Almost immediately it moved inward to reveal Lavon Gatling.

"Come in, come in. I've been ex*pect*ing you." An engaging smile enclosed by a perfect parentheses of dimples welcomed them. Their hostess was now more suitably dressed, for which at least part of Poppy was relieved. The part that had to think.

The room they entered was cool. Floor tiles echoed a marimba-like rhythm as Lavon Gatling's high heels clicked against them. She looked, Poppy thought, like Grace Kelly, *except for all that piled up, platinum-blonde Dolly-hair.* Her light gray suit was professional and neat, and she had somehow managed to downplay the impact of her bosom by covering it with a white, ruffled blouse. She turned, activating the dimples again. "I've made some lemonade." She gestured toward a low table where a tray held a sweating crystal pitcher and three tall glasses.

They sat in wicker chairs near a sun-splashed corner where dozens of potted plants vied for the light. Dark green leaves rose behind Lavon Gatling, a perfect frame for her pose. Poppy took a deep breath and began. "Miz Stoner and I are private investigators working for Lil Turnbow. The women at Hallelujah Bend don't believe Christine Jessup's death was an accident."

The woman across the table leaned toward Poppy and spoke in a straightforward manner. "I really ad*mire* those women out there by the river, and if it matters, I'm *very* comfortable with the fact that they are lesbians. Live and let live, I say."

Hmmm, W.C. Does "comfortable" include being wrapped around Lil like a python?

Lavon Gatling continued, "Do they think someone actually *murdered* Christine? She was such a pretty little thing . . . and so im*pass*ioned, too. The Save the River group will really feel her loss."

Belle opened a small tablet and tapped a pen against it. This had the apparent desired result on Poppy. She blinked and squared her shoulders. "There seem to be a lot of people who stand to profit if the river is dammed, Miz Gatling. It does seem that a formal investigation into Christine Jessup's death should have been considered."

Lavon Gatling's eyebrows rose in tandem as she answered, "My husband *did* go to the scene. There was nothing there to indicate *any*thing, except that she fell from the cliff, struck her head and then drowned in the river below." She turned to glance coolly at Belle, then returned her gaze to Poppy. "Have you found anything to the *cont*rary?" A tiny muscle in the lower lid of Lavon Gatling's left eye had begun to tense, causing the lashes to quiver.

"Yes," Poppy replied. "We have. But we won't reveal anything until we complete our investigation." She leaned forward in her chair and placed her glass of lemonade on the tray. She rose and looked down at their hostess. "Thank you for your time, Miz Gatling. Will we see you at the town meeting tonight?"

Lavon Gatling stood and nodded. "I'll be giving a short talk."

Belle had moved toward a doorway which opened off away from the direction they had come in. She pointed, asking, "Is this your office? It must be nice to work from your home."

"Yes, it is." Lavon Gatling walked into the room, flicking on a light. "This is where I spend a *lot* of my time, I'm afraid." She waved her hand in an expansive gesture, encompassing the whole room.

Poppy followed her into the spacious office. She

noticed a stack of orange brochures on a coffee table. The Bosco Bluffs logo caught her eye. She thought the brothers Bosco must be dead certain the lake was going to be a reality and wondered at the blind arrogance of some people. A low sofa filled one whole wall of the room, a map of Hermosa County above it. Poppy remembered Pete's comment about the Sheriff's wife spending a lot of time "on her back." *Well, W.C., we've heard of casting couches . . . s'pose that's the sales sofa?*

Belle asked, looking at a wall covered with snapshots of airplanes. "Do you fly?"

"It's my greatest passion." Lavon Gatling pointed to a poster-size photograph of a sleek Beech Bonanza F33A. "This is my sweetheart, *Plane Jane.*"

Poppy leaned forward to get a better look. Lavon Gatling stepped in close behind her, pressing her body against Poppy's backside from knee to waist. She pointed past Poppy's ear, her bosom brushing softly along Poppy's arm as she spoke. "See there." A long red fingernail clicked against the glass over the aircraft's wing where a tall man stood, his hat raised in salute. "That's Troy." She leaned away and stepped backward. "Poor baby, *he* won't get off the ground, but . . ." Lavon Gatling looked directly into Poppy's eyes. "Thank goodness, *I've* never had a fear of flying."

The syrup-waffle routine had its way with Papillon Audubon Dillworth as she tried to gather poise enough to speak. She had the sensation of experiencing a near-miss with a Mack truck.

Belle rescued her — sort of. "How nice for you. Poppy flies, too. But never without her co-pilot . . .

me." Belle slipped her hand around Poppy's elbow and squeezed.

Move over, Kali. Ole blue-eyes is gonna be sleeping on the porch for sure, now. "Harumph." *Almost there, Wondercrone. Keep chuggin'.* "Well. Uh . . . We've got to be going now." Poppy made her knees work and walked toward the doorway. She felt the full force of Lavon Gatling's megawatt smile behind her, dimples activated, eyes smoldering, as she and Belle emerged into the stuffy afternoon.

"Well," Belle said as the door closed behind them. "That woman certainly has a way about her, doesn't she, dear?"

Poppy was pretty sure this was another one of those questions which was better off without an answer. She smiled at Belle and squeezed her hand. She yawned as the effect of the heat made itself known. A cool nap suddenly seemed like a marvelous idea. The evening ahead could turn into a late one. The coming town meeting loomed in her mind as they drove back to Hallelujah Bend.

CHAPTER FIVE
Tom's Discovery

Just after sunset, Poppy and Belle, as napped and refreshed as the cabin air conditioner would permit, sat at the rear of the main auditorium of the Pecan Valley High School. Lil had given an impassioned speech for saving the river and Lavon Gatling was just finishing what had been a surprisingly eloquent plea for the people of Hermosa County to pull together and do the "right thing."

That being, Poppy supposed, anything that would put dollars into Lavon Gatling's beaded clutch bag.

The most fun Poppy had experienced in a while happened next when Ned Bosco came to the microphone to speak and the sound equipment mysteriously stopped working. He shouted and croaked into a cheerleader's megaphone while the audience tittered. Poppy had earlier seen Melvin Mossbacker's van in the parking lot. She searched the crowd for a sight of him. He came up behind her, smiling like a Cheshire cat, his receding hairline almost a halo above his innocent expression.

She grinned at him, her eyebrows raised. "You didn't have anything to do with this spectacle, did you?"

"The Goddess lives. Her name is Ralph." He sidled off toward the stage saying happily, "I'm next up. See ya."

Melvin Mossbacker, with a now-working microphone, gave a rousing and factually sound talk on the environmental issues at hand. Poppy was counting and she was happy to calculate that he got more hurrahs than boos. Perhaps the river would live after all.

When the meeting was over Poppy remained standing, watching the interactions between some of the prime players in the game she was trying to understand. Her gaze at the moment was still on Lavon Gatling. Poppy had watched her conclude the town meeting and leave the stage to re-emerge in the crowd of people who loitered, talking, between the stage and front row of seats. Tyrone Needham and his wife Gloria were conversing earnestly with Lavon Gatling when Poppy noticed Lil and Marsha and Marsha's son, Tom Ross, making their way up the crowded aisle toward her.

She acknowledged Lil's wave with a nod and looked back at Lavon Gatling, who was now standing momentarily alone. Poppy was surprised to see that Tom Ross had gone back to speak to her. He seemed to say just a few words, then turned to follow his mother and her lover.

Poppy watched Lavon Gatling's eyes follow young Tom's red head until he joined Poppy and the other two women. Poppy made a mental note that the famous Gatling dimples were at half-mast and a few teeth were showing.

Marsha Needham stood beside Lil, her hand resting lightly on Lil's arm. Poppy saw a tiny muscle tense in Marsha's jaw as Gloria Needham passed by not two feet away without speaking to her sister. Poppy noted Gloria's husband was no longer at her side. *Say now, where's that banker got off to?* Poppy located Tyrone Needham, again in conversation with Lavon Gatling, whose dimples were now in full *off* position and the only teeth showing were those of the tiger mascot on the shield above the stage.

About an hour later, they were all gathered around the large oval table in the dining room at Hallelujah Bend. The day was rapidly turning into the late evening which Poppy had earlier dreaded. Juno and Kali had retired to Juno's room upstairs, but all the adult members of the women's camp were still wide awake. Lovey and Pete were sitting in the Mom and Pop chairs at either end of the table. Poppy and Belle were seated along one side while Lil and Marsha and Tom Ross were scooted up to the other side.

It seemed odd to Poppy to see a man in the room, but Tom Ross sat between his mother and Lil, with a piece of paper in his hand which had obviously been torn from a spiral notebook. Poppy noted the paper was quivering as he began to speak. "Mother." He turned to face Marsha. "You know I'd been seeing a lot of Chris, but I don't think the rest of you knew it. Except for Lovey, who promised she wouldn't say anything until Chris and I were ready to make it public." He darted a look down the table at Lovey, who nodded her white head sagely. "See, I started out working on the laker side of this business, but when I got to know Chris, everything changed." His voice faltered and he swallowed hard. Poppy noticed he had made a fist of his free hand and the knuckles of it had whitened as his discomfort grew.

Marsha patted her son's arm. "I'm sorry, Tom . . . *very* sorry Christine died. You really came to care for her, didn't you?"

"Yeah, I did." He cleared his throat. "I fell for her pretty hard. I'd never met anyone like her." He was obviously having trouble controlling his emotions and he cleared his throat again. "If she hadn't been so damned wrapped up in all this Save the River business, she might still be alive."

Poppy spoke up. "Why do you think that, son?"

Tom Ross looked up at Poppy and said gruffly, "Because she told me she was frightened. Someone killed one of her cats and put it in her mailbox . . .

and she said someone had been prowling around the Springs."

"She say who it was?"

"No. She never saw them. It was always at night . . . she got hang-up calls at night, too."

Lil leaned forward. "That sounds like a deliberate campaign to terrorize that young woman!"

The young man nodded and turned his attention back to the piece of paper in his hand. "She wrote things down in a journal, too." He looked up. "This is not from that, though. I looked for the journal but I didn't find it."

Belle said, "So that's what you were doing at the Springs yesterday morning. You were the one who tossed Chris's room, weren't you?

Tossed. Hey-hey, Dillworth. Our partner's learning this Private Eye lingo pretty fast. Musta been doing her studying. Poppy watched Tom Ross closely, her curiosity rising about the nature of the page he held. She wondered when he had found it and how long he had had it. She heard what he was saying, but a part of her mind wanted to know what he was *not* saying.

"Yeah. That was me up at the Springs. But, I didn't find this in the house. I found it in the glove box of her car where it's parked inside the barn." He flattened the page against the tabletop.

Pete leaned forward, sputtering with impatience. "Well, speak louder, boy. What the hell is it? Spit it out. I'm gonna pass on from old age before long."

Tom Ross smiled weakly. "It's a will. Chris made a hand-written will giving everything she had to Lil to help save the river and to fund the Cronesnest project that Lovey's been working on." He pushed the paper toward Lil's hand on the table. "Here," he said into the hushed silence. "Read it."

Hoooboy. This case is trying to solve itself, W.C. . . . But . . . now it's gonna look like the number one best suspect is sitting there with the motive in her hand!

Lil read aloud, with tremulous voice, "*I, Naomi Christine Jessup, state that I am of sane mind and sound body and that I wish upon fact of my death, that all of my earthly estate and holdings be given to Lillian Turnbow to help in the fight to save the river and other Hallelujah Bend projects, specifically Cronesnest, a retirement home for older women. This is my last will and testament.*" Lil turned toward Marsha. "She's signed it and the date is June the twenty-eighth, this year . . ." She reached up for the Alison Bechdel calendar beside the doorway and turned back a page. "My God. That was the day before she died."

Lovey stood at the end of the table, one hand braced against the chair back, the other at her throat, fingers fluttering. Her eyes widened behind the thick lenses of her spectacles. "Is that piece of paper legal? Could it really be true?"

Marsha took the page from Lil and looked closely at it. "I think it is. I believe a handwritten will is legal — in Texas, at least." She looked meaningfully at Lil. "We'll have to take this to Dallas and get Sylvia to take a look at it. This is definitely something for an attorney to handle — and I don't trust anyone in Hermosa County."

"Yeah . . . right." Lil slid down in her chair, seeming to melt against it, then she popped upright, galvanized by what Poppy guessed was her next thought. "We've got to be *extremely* careful. This piece of paper can mean the answer to a lot of things. It *could* save our blessed river. And —" She looked at Lovey who was again seated. "Lovey, it *could* mean the fulfillment of your dream for Cronesnest . . . but, first we need to check its legality, and then we must get it legally registered or something."

Poppy spoke up. "Tomorrow's Independence Day, too. Everything'll be closed up tighter'n a deacon's hatband."

"Shit," Lil exclaimed, then went on pensively. "Yeah — and tomorrow's the last big chance for speeches and politicking before the election. I really think a lot of folks are on our side, too." She looked at Marsha. "Marsha and I are the two main speakers for Save the River tomorrow, and Marsha's friends from her years in the Senate crowd are coming up from Austin."

Tom Ross' deep voice rumbled. "Mother, can't you and Lil go ahead and call your attorney tonight, then put the will somewhere safe until you can get to Dallas with it?"

Lil nodded agreement. "We'll have to. I can't think of any better idea . . ." She looked around the table. "Can any of you?"

Poppy couldn't. She observed each of the others. Lovey and Pete seemed to be in a state of euphoria and Belle slowly wagged her head in a *no* direction.

Poppy thought of tomorrow and hoped that skyrockets and firecrackers would be the most exciting part of their day.

CHAPTER SIX
Fireworks

July the Fourth, always hot in Texas, had not disappointed anyone. The bank thermometer had registered ninety-four degrees at eleven-thirty A.M. as the last of the parade floats passed by. Now, at seven P.M., after the contents of bowls and jars and red-and-white buckets had travelled from the long tables into the stomachs of Hermosa County's finest, the temperature had risen to one hundred and six degrees.

The humidity was high, the air so heavy it seemed to rest against Poppy's skin. The only cloud she had seen all day was the gnats above the barrel of watermelon rinds. Even the children, usually manic on any holiday, were subdued and lay about on the grass, too hot even to pick at each other.

Lovey and Pete had set up a table in the concession area, hawking herbs, honey, jelly, chow-chow relish and Pete's *Hot Sauce From Hell.*

Juno sat by Poppy's feet, seemingly content to pull all the red threads, one by one, from a small flag, transforming it into an oddly pleasing pink, white and blue. Juno, like the other children, also seemed subdued, but Poppy thought it was probably more from Lil's speech, rather than from the heat.

The impact of Lil's revelation had sobered quite a few people. Lil, in her fervor, had not been able to keep quiet about Christine Jessup's will and had informed the crowd of supporters and foes alike that the Mother had come to the earth's rescue and the consolidation of Jessup land and money with Turnbow land and energy would make a formidable obstacle against those who wanted to kill the river.

Poppy wished for a nap and a snuggle with Belle, but she thought she should stay and observe the actions of the major players in the mystery she was here to solve. Her knees ached from standing too long and then from sitting too long on the hard park benches. She watched Belle and Juno as they rose to go and play the baseball and ring-toss games that were set up in the shade of the old pecan trees. Poppy begged off to stay behind and think for a while about the events of the past few days and how they fit together.

And how they did not.

She sat on a shaded bench and tried to make sense of what she had learned so far. She believed Chris Jessup had been murdered. And that the murderer was most likely someone with a lot to gain if the river was dammed and the Hermosa valley flooded by a lake. A lake which seemed to offer as many solutions as it did problems. But many folks would gain. Especially those like the Boscos who had already invested heavily.

Was Marsha's son, Tom Ross, really all he appeared to be? His anger at his mother over her new lifestyle seemed to have evaporated rather easily. Could he and Chris have had a lover's quarrel? And what of others in Hermosa county? Were all the players on stage in this little drama, or was someone hiding in the wings?

Poppy's mind and heart would not allow her even to consider Lil as a suspect. Though the Sheriff was sure to see it that way now that news was out about Chris's will. In fact, Poppy thought, Sheriff Gatling would now probably be *very* interested in re-opening the investigation of Chris's death. His wife would be certain to see this new turn of events as a means of discrediting the Save the River group. Who but Lil would now seem to have the most to gain from Chris's death?

Poppy had seen Lavon Gatling off and on all day, first in the midst of one group, then another, her dimpled smile as bright as the sun reflecting from her silvery, upswept hair. A woman who perhaps wasn't what she seemed? Or maybe was *more* than she seemed? She was indeed someone who stood to gain from the success of the lake. But how much luxury could a person want? Lavon Gatling appeared to already have much more than enough. Was her need for more dollars strong enough to cause her to murder someone who stood in the way of her desires?

The Pecan Valley State Bank was certainly pro-lake. Did that mean anything other than what was dictated by the common sense of commerce? That an economic boom would indeed come about? Though the lake was *ecologically* undesirable, the fact remained that a lake would bring new people, new business, new money. All *good* for a bank. *Better for a failing bank than for a sound one, Wondercrone? Or should we say, better for the banker?* Poppy resolved to find out more about Mr. Tyrone Needham and the state of his financial affairs.

Melvin Mossbacker had stopped by for a while and accompanied Poppy and Belle to watch Sheriff Gatling cast a rubber plug through a hoop. When the Sheriff asked for challengers, Poppy had, much to Melvin's gleeful surprise, beaten the Sheriff with a score of ten for ten. They had stayed and watched the two Bosco brothers. Both of them had been busy as raccoons at a minnow farm, though each had directed similar baleful looks at Poppy and Belle and their companion. Melvin had left early, saying he hated to have fun while Ralph was working hard at his job as a ranger at the state park.

Day was rapidly growing into evening when Poppy's musing was interrupted by the return of Belle and of Juno, who tugged at her arm excitedly. "Poppy — Poppy. Come *on*. We gotta get a good seat for the fireworks."

The leprechaun in Poppy's heart began to dance in rhythm with the jigging girl in front of her. The only thing Poppy liked better than being a lesbian was fireworks. "Awright! You don't have to tell me twice. Lead me to 'em." She walked faster than her knees wanted to go but not nearly as fast as her memories prompted. To sit high in the grandstands with the woman she loved, on a summer night in Texas and let the girl inside her sing ooohs and aaahs in chorus with her young friend close by — whizzers and Roman candles and rockets and sparklers . . . *Yeppers, W.C., the only thing missing is a good dog.*

Later, still aglow from the fireworks but tired and anticipating a good night's sleep, Poppy pulled the Trooper up last in the caravan back to Hallelujah Bend. Juno was asleep on the back seat and Belle was nodding beside Poppy in the front. Poppy couldn't resist. "Hey!" Belle's head popped up. "No fair sleeping there, co-pilot." Belle grinned sheepishly.

They followed Pete and Lovey in Pete's ancient pickup. Lil and Marsha led the way in the pink Continental. Poppy's radar kicked in as they drove through the gate. "That's funny. The gate was open. Pete must be getting forgetful. Or Lovey. They've always been real careful about locking up when everyone's gone at the same time."

The same concerns must have been felt by the occupants of the other two vehicles, because they speeded up, leaving the Trooper behind. Poppy goosed the pedal a little, jostling Juno awake. Just then Poppy noticed the guard light was out and the farmhouse was completely dark.

"Belle," Poppy said levelly. "Open the glove box and hand me the flashlight and my pistol."

She saw Pete's truck and Marsha's Continental parked in front with the doors left opened. The women had already gone inside. *Godamighty, those women need a lesson in caution!* Poppy brought the Trooper to a sliding stop and reached for the items Belle held out. She opened the door and was on the ground before her knees could complain.

"Be careful, Papillon."

"I will, hon," Poppy answered.

Juno crawled out of the vehicle and stood beside Belle, rubbing her eyes. "Where's Kali?" She looked anxiously around. "Here girl, heeere Kali. C'mon girl." Juno whistled loudly, putting both her little fingers to the corners of her mouth. But Kali didn't appear.

Poppy's heart lurched as she saw the house light up. Lil stood on the porch, pushing shells into a shotgun. She clicked the firearm shut and shouted at Poppy. "Somebody's broken in! The place is wrecked! Juno, come up here with me!"

Juno started to whistle again.

"*Now,* Juno." Lil's voice was strained. "Kali's probably after a gopher. C'mon now."

Poppy and Belle walked with Juno to the porch, releasing her to Lil's protective arm. Poppy said, "Belle and I'll check the outside while y'all do the inside. Be *careful,* Lil. Someone could still be in there." She slipped her .38 Police Special from its holster and released the cylinder, checking its load. Satisfied, she clicked it closed and motioned for Belle to stay close.

She aimed the flashlight up at the pole where the guard light hung. It had been shattered. *Careful Dillworth . . . That light had to have been shot out.* Her chest squeezed as she thought immediately of the missing dog. *Nope — Nopers. Won't think about that. Not yet.* She breathed deeply, trying to calm the anxiety-activated thumping of her heart.

She heard the click behind her of Belle's pistol as Belle apparently went through the routine Poppy had just completed. It heartened Poppy to remember all the practicing they had done at the shooting range. A beam of light from Belle's powerful flashlight illuminated a part of the yard to Poppy's left.

Belle said softly, "Okay, Pardner. Let's go."

They made their way cautiously around the side of the old house and around the corner toward the screened-in back porch. They saw it at the same time. "Uh-oh," Poppy said.

Belle spoke. "Uh-huh. Looks like this is how they got in."

Poppy crept slowly up the steps toward the door where a splintered doorjamb gave evidence of forced entry.

"Be careful, Poppy. They could be hiding on the porch."

"Okay," Poppy answered as she gingerly pulled the screen door open. "I don't think so, though. There's no vehicle here and there wouldn't have been any reason to open the gate if the perp was on foot —" Poppy lost her hold on the door handle and jumped back in fright as a figure loomed in the doorway.

"Hey! Dillworth!" Pete shouted down at Poppy as she turned on the porch light. "C'mon in here and look at this mess."

"Jesusmaryandjoseph, Pete!" Poppy angrily pushed her glasses up to ride atop her head. "You old fool. You might not get the *chance* to die of old age if you keep doing things like *that*. There's two pistols out here, you know."

"*Two* guns, you say? Whaddaya need *two* for?" Pete peered into the night. "Oh, yeah. I see . . . *Her.* I didn't know you allowed *her* to pack a gun, too."

"Now see here, Odessa Peters," Poppy began, "*her* name is B —"

Pete shouted louder, her hearing apparently unaided again. "I *said*, come on in here. It's a *mess*."

The door shut in Poppy's face as Pete disappeared, leaving Poppy sputtering on the steps. "Why that old —"

"Don't worry about it, honey," Belle murmured. "She's just excited."

"Hmph. Excited? I'm gonna show her *excited*. I *know* she saw my lips moving. She's not *blind*." Poppy yanked open the door, fully prepared to pin her old friend's defective ears to the wall. She stopped as Belle placed a hand firmly on her arm.

"It'll work out, Papillon . . . Please. This isn't the time or the place."

Poppy took a deep breath. Her heart pounded with a tympanic rhythm. "Whew," she said, expelling a rush of air. "Okay, Belle. I'll let it be . . . For now. But, sooner or later I'm gonna set Pete straight."

They entered the house and Poppy thought that Pete was right about one thing. The place *was* a mess. Drawers were pulled out and dumped on the floor. Papers and books were scattered, chairs and even the sofa had been ripped and turned over. Someone had made a thorough, systematic search of the house, room by room. Upstairs the beds were tossed about, mattresses askew.

Poppy stood in the doorway to Juno's room where Lil sat on the floor beside her daughter, holding her as she sobbed. "Oh, Mama. I just know something's happened to Kali." Juno looked up, red-eyed, at Poppy. "She wouldna let a burglar do all this. She woulda tried to stop him." She turned her face back toward Lil's bosom, her shoulders heaving as she wailed louder.

Lil looked across Juno's head at Poppy. She didn't have to say anything. Poppy could see agreement in her eyes. Lil said, "I'm sure whoever did this was after the will . . . but it wasn't even here. It was in the trunk of the car all along."

When sleep finally came that night for Poppy, it was fitful and punctuated by dreams of her old job as a sheriff's clerk. There were no keys on her typewriter and she couldn't find any paper and when she found the paper and rolled it into the old Underwood, the sheets turned into corn shucks covered with bits of greasy tamale. Only when Belle finally snuggled close to Poppy's back did she sleep soundly, her heart beating a soft, strong rhythm.

CHAPTER SEVEN
Doggone

Morning became electric as the travel-alarm went off, sending a buzzing tremor along Poppy's neck. She reached for it stiffly, her fingers tingling as they strove to follow the rest of her body into wakefulness. Her mouth was dry, her sinuses stuffy and her head pounded from too little sleep. She rubbed her forehead and gazed fondly at Belle who still slept beside her, her lower lip making *miffle* sounds as she breathed. She leaned close and kissed her on the cheek. The *miffing* stopped and Belle opened her eyes.

"Mmmph," Belle said. "Teef." She pointed to the cup on the bedside table. Poppy handed it to her and watched as Belle deftly retrieved her bridge and clicked it into place. "Mornin', sweet Mariposa," she said, teeth and smile now firmly in place.

"You too, darlin'."

"Does it feel hot in here to you, Poppy?" Belle dabbed her damp temples with the hem of her sleeveless tee shirt. "It's been years since I had a hot flash, but that's what I feel like."

"Yeppers. It's hot. That poor little air conditioner's been floggin' itself all night, but the humidity is still stifling. Bet today's gonna be a steamer. The way my knees are acting, I'd say we're in for some rain too, and pretty soon." She rolled toward Belle, "It's too hot for snuggles, but I gotta have a hug." She pressed close inside Belle's embrace and soaked up as much comfort as she could before she had to come up for air. Then she wrapped her arms around Belle's narrow shoulders and hugged her firmly for a moment. "I love you, Belle," she whispered. "It's wonderful waking up beside you every morning."

Belle answered, "Me, too, you," sliding her free hand along Poppy's thigh. "I'm getting lonesome for something more than hugs, though. How 'bout you?"

"Mmmm-hmmm. We'll have to find time pretty soon. Might forget how if we wait too long. But —" Poppy rose and headed for the shower. "It'll have to wait a little longer, 'cause we have some tough chores to do this morning." She remembered one in particular. "Wonder if Kali ever showed up last night?"

Belle swung her legs over the side of the bed. "I hope so . . . Juno was so upset when we left. I know just how she feels, too." She looked thoughtfully out the window. "I had Daisy. A wonderful old mare. I *still* get choked up when I remember the day I lost her."

Poppy came back to sit on the edge of the bed by Belle. She hugged her shoulders. "I know, hon. I know . . . and I'm really worried about Kali, too."

They rose together and walked, holding hands, into the tiny bathroom. Poppy stepped into the ancient shower, looking first for waterbugs. "Come on in here. There's *no* hot water and only cold water enough in the tank for two if we share the shower." She stepped into the spray. "Whoooeee! This'll cool us off in a hurry."

Belle joined her, shivering, sliding into the slippery circle of Poppy's soapy arms. "I don't know, darling," she said as she moved like a dolphin against Poppy's body. "It might just warm us up."

A half hour later, Poppy and Belle sat with the others around the oval table in the dining room of the purple farmhouse. The kitchen was now a neat oasis in an otherwise jumbled house. Dishes and coffee cups clanged as the women finished breakfast. Pete, who had been silent during the meal, now spoke out loudly. "Almost shot me last night, Dillworth. That's all them guns are good for. Hear about it all the time. Accidental shootings."

Poppy growled, "I'm surprised you ever hear about anything, you old geezer."

"Teasin'?" Pete glowered at Poppy. "I ain't teasin', I'm dead serious."

"You're dead from the neck up, idjut. I said *geezer!"* Poppy jumped as Belle kicked her ankle.

Lovey sighed and patted Pete's breast pocket, then did a Carol Burnett tug on her ear.

"Oh." Pete reddened and pulled a dime-sized, flesh colored hearing-aid from her pocket. She poked it in her ear and pulled her hat brim down over her eyes.

Poppy leaned forward and said loudly, *"Welcome aboard!"*

Pete jumped. "You don't have to shout, Dillworth. I ain't deaf, ya know."

Poppy grinned in spite of herself, then turned to the subject on all of their minds. "How do you plan to handle this business, Lil? You gonna report it to the Sheriff?"

"Yeah. We'll do that first. Would you go with us, Poppy? I'd like for you to be there. Then we'll be off to Dallas, to get that will to a safer place."

Lil turned to look out the window at Juno. The girl sat twirling slowly in a tire that was swinging from a limb of a giant pecan tree. "Juno was so distraught I thought she'd *never* go to sleep last night, and when she found out Kali wasn't here this morning — well, she's just been sitting out there. She won't eat. I don't know what to do. She wants to go look for her." Lil turned her attention back to the cup of coffee in front of her. "I really fear the worst about Kali." She made a fist with her free hand. "What kind of crazy bastard would kill a kid's dog?"

Belle asked softly. "Would it help if I stayed with Juno today?" She looked at Poppy, who nodded her agreement. "We might at least look around here. We *might* even find her . . . alive, hopefully."

Lil smiled gratefully. "It sure would be a help, Belle. Juno seems to've really taken to you, anyhow."

Pete rose stiffly. "Think I'll take a look around the catfish ponds and down by the gardens. Seems I ain't needed here." She stalked from the table and out the door, then turned back to say, "Besides, I'm going to get those two cats from over at the Springs and bring 'em back here. I think we got rats."

Sonavgun, W.C. When a dog-woman like P.A. Dillworth owns up to having a cat, it opens up all sorts of possibilities. Looks like old Petey's trying to buy some affection. And, Poppy thought, that probably wasn't a bad thing, considering the looks of happy approval on the faces of both Lovey and Belle.

Lovey, in pleased surprise at this turn in Pete's behavior, sighed as the door slammed. "Can you have menopause twice? I think Pete's on her second trip." She began to clear the table. "I'll stay here at the house and see if I can put some more of this stuff to rights."

Marsha, who'd been very quiet, said, "They were looking for that will, weren't they, Lil? It had to be someone we saw yesterday at the park. Someone standing in the crowd when you announced the will's existence." She took Lil's hand with her long slender fingers and raised it to her lips. "We must be very careful, sweetheart. Someone around here has gone completely over the edge."

Lil nodded thoughtfully. "I'm glad we just got that last lot of finished figures to the gallery. They played hell up at the studio, too. My tools are thrown all over and the new Hecate I just started no longer has a nose."

Marsha's eyes grew large as Lil talked. Her hair swung forward as she leaned close to Lil's shoulder. Suddenly Marsha squared her shoulders and swept her hair back with both hands, retying it in back with a turquoise scarf. "I'd like to get my hands on whoever it was." Her eyes glistened with emotion. "I've just about had it with this town!"

A little later, after a frustrating and pointless visit with Sheriff Gatling, Poppy and Lil and Marsha sat in Marsha's comfortable Lincoln in the bank parking lot. Though they were parked in the shade of the covered spaces reserved for bank officials, they had all the doors open, trying to catch any breeze that happened to move. The air was heavy with the promise of rain.

Lil grumbled, "I should've known better than to expect the Sheriff to be of much help."

Marsha agreed, fuming. "And to have him turn the whole thing upside down like that. The very idea. *Now* he wants to launch a full-scale investigation into Christine's death. Now that he thinks it would give the Save the River group a black eye." Marsha crossed her arms over her middle, angrily holding each elbow. "I'll wager Gunner is having a multiple orgasm over all this."

Poppy spoke up from the back seat. "I was afraid the Sheriff would try to turn the discovery of the will to his advantage . . . or *their* advantage, I should say." She looked at her watch. "It's almost nine-thirty. Are you sure your brother-in-law always follows the same routine?"

"Mm-hmm, see." Marsha nodded toward a low Mercedes which had just slunk onto the lot. "Here he comes."

Poppy watched as Tyrone Needham apparently saw them and braked to a stop, then began to roll forward again and parked beside the Continental.

"Is this a stick-up?" he asked as he closed his car door and walked toward them, smiling, his eyelids puffy and pale.

Poppy noticed Marsha's knuckles whiten as she gripped the steering wheel. Obviously Marsha was not amused at her brother-in-law's attempt at humor.

Lil came around to lean against the fender as she spoke. "No. It's not a stick-up, Needham." She cracked the knuckles of one hand as she spoke and Tyrone Needham blinked delicately at each snap. "But we're on a tight schedule. Didn't want to chance missing you."

"All right." He jammed his hands into his trouser pockets. "What is it then? Let's get it over with."

"I want to know how soon I can withdraw money from the Jessup estate. With the election only ten days away, I need to get at it as soon as possible in order to put it to work the way Chris wanted."

The banker's eyebrows came down into the hint of a frown. "That's something for the legal department to handle, Ms. Turnbow. I have great doubts as to the authenticity of that rumored will, anyway."

"Oh, it's authentic, all right, Needham. And if I have to —" She glanced at Marsha. "With Marsha's help, I'll get the fastest court order in the history of jurisprudence. You can expect to see me at the teller's window very soon."

Tyrone Needham's handsome face seemed to sag and his upper lip had taken on a grayish tone. "It's the bank's duty to protect that money. I was named the executor of Emory Jessup's estate and I see it as my *personal* duty to his memory to see to it that not one dollar *ever* goes to you . . ." He glanced toward the car where Marsha sat, then back at Lil. "Or anyone *like* you."

Lil stood up straight, almost as tall as the man facing her and fully as broad across the shoulders. "You seem to have forgotten something. That estate belonged to Christine Jessup. Her father left it to her. He's been dead for a year. It was Chris's to do with as she saw fit. And she saw fit to give it to *me!*" Lil leaned toward Needham as she spoke.

The banker stepped backward, clearly disturbed by Lil's tirade.

Lil continued, "Why are you so nervous, Needham?" She stepped toward him. "Did a few of Preacher Jessup's dollars find their way into *your* pocket?"

"Wait a minute. You can't talk to me like that. This conversation is ov—." He stopped speaking suddenly as Lavon Gatling's white Jeep rolled slowly past the parking lot entrance. He turned back to Lil, visibly shaken. "I must go in now. Goodbye." He turned and hurried into the bank.

Marsha was the first to speak. "He's such a pompous asshole. I'll *never* know why Gloria stays with him. But, I've known Ty since we were kids, and he's always been like that. Never wants to face anything head on. Always hiding behind rules and laws."

Poppy had seen Lavon Gatling's vehicle almost stop, then move on down the street out of sight. She didn't think the other two women had seen it. Now she saw it again as Lavon had evidently circled the block. This time it turned into the lot. "Uh-oh," Poppy said. "We got company."

The Jeep came even with the rear end of the Lincoln and stopped. The tinted window on the driver's side came down. Lavon Gatling said brightly, "What's going on? Do you ladies need some help?" She batted her lashes.

Lil answered, "No, Gunner. Everything's right on schedule. We're just robbing the bank, that's all. It should blow any minute. You can go on in, if you want . . . otherwise move along. You're blocking our getaway."

Lavon Gatling smiled sweetly, her dimples deepening, and slowly raised the window. The Jeep leaped forward, scratching dust and gravel into the sweltering air. Poppy watched as it careened onto the street, antennas whipping.

Hmmm, W.C. Kinda nosy ain't she. Maybe she's propped those hooters on old Tyrone's chest a couple times. He skittered off like a stump-shy heifer.

As Marsha nosed the Lincoln off the lot, Poppy

noticed a big black stretch-cab Chevy pickup pull in and park. A sign on the side said *Bosco Bluffs Marina*. She watched with growing interest as the brothers got out and walked toward the doorway the banker had gone through. *Hmmm, W.C. Looks like all the players are on stage this morning.*

Aloud Poppy said, "You women better get that will on into town A.S.A.P." Her thought turned to Belle and Juno and their quest. "And you can drop me off at the camp on the way. I'm kinda anxious to see if Kali's turned up."

Lil nodded, saying, "Yeah. Me too, Poppy."

Poppy looked up at the sky. "Weather gal's predicting storms for this afternoon, too." She rubbed her knee. "My bones are saying she's right, too. Y'all be careful in town now."

CHAPTER EIGHT
The River Rises

Poppy sat alone on the front porch of the purple farmhouse. Lil and Marsha had left for Dallas an hour ago. The valley now echoed with constant booms of thunder as the line of storms moved in from the southwest.

Belle had gone upstairs with Juno to comfort and console the girl. Though they had searched diligently all morning, they had turned up no trace of the black Labrador.

Poppy watched as the sky in the southwest rapidly filled with the popcorn tops of thunderheads. The clouds rose separately, but in a line like marching men, as the severe weather front moved closer. The air was sticky and still and the sauna-like heat made it difficult to breathe. The television weatherwoman had announced that the area was under a flash-flood watch and a tornado warning. The *warning* part disturbed Poppy. That meant one or more tornadoes had been sighted and confirmed by the ground radar, somewhere in the area. In this case a particularly prankish tornado had skipped through Four Corners, a tiny town in the next county, wiping out its only reason for existence — three package liquor stores and a honkeytonk. Poppy could already see the lips of fundamentalists everywhere forming the words, *God's will.*

Belle returned and joined Poppy on the porch swing. They held hands, quietly communing, waiting for the weather to hit. Belle murmured, "Juno's napping, poor child."

Poppy nodded, then pointed toward the hill on the other side of the river. "Look! You can see the down-draft from the storm. Wow! Look at those trees lay down."

The leaves on the trees in the front yard began to dance as the groundswell of dust rolled toward them. Then the cold force of the storm's breath pressed against the earth and everything that wasn't nailed down began to flap and screech and pinwheel across the yard. The trees dipped and swayed and Poppy felt the grit pecking against her glasses, tasted it in her mouth. She felt Belle snuggling close to her side, but she couldn't go in. Not yet.

This part of a storm always excited her. The ionized air made her want to dash around the yard in dog-circles before the cooling rains came.

The sky darkened and took on a greenish glow as the heavy skeins of rain became visible beneath the rumbling clouds. The down-draft calmed as quickly as it had come and several fat raindrops splatted against the dust. Small powdery puffs rose from the driveway as if it were pelted by bullets.

"Great Hera! Look at that." Poppy pointed toward the barbed wire fence along the drive. It glowed and popped with energy as tiny balls of electricity rolled from it, landing smoking on the grass. Poppy remembered what the phenomenon meant, but not before she could get her hands to her ears. A sudden cannon shot of thunder rattled her lungs and the world lost all its color. Everything turned white as lightning buzzed like a million bees down the rooster's tail on the weathervane atop the tall corner fence pole.

Every hair on Poppy's body stood at attention. She grabbed Belle, her heart pounding. The door flew open behind them as Pete and Lovey came onto the porch. Lovey's hand was over her heart and Pete was holding her fedora, eyes wide with shock. Poppy tapped something within herself which could have become hysteria in a lesser woman and shouted at Pete. "Well, didja hear *that*, Petey?"

Pete blinked a couple of times, then grinned at Poppy. "Yeah. I *can* hear thunder . . . you old fart."

"Listen!" Poppy cupped her hand to her best ear.

"What's that?" She rose and walked toward the front steps. A faint whimper came from somewhere below her. "Kali!" She lurched down the steps, her knees grinding painfully as she knelt and peered into the gloom beneath the porch.

"Ow." Poppy jumped as a hailstone hit her shoulder. Loud cracks and pops sounded as hail began to hit the roof. She looked up at Belle. *It's now — or wait till after the storm, W.C.* "Somebody get me a flashlight. I'm going under there." Poppy saw Belle leap into action and head for the house. She tuned out the pain as her bare knees pressed against pebbles and clods while she crept into the blackness.

"Here girl." She pursed her lips and made kissing noises, calling to the dog. "Where are you, Kali? C'mon, talk to me, girl."

A weak whine sounded from somewhere deeper under the house. She heard Belle's footsteps above her, then felt the cold of the flashlight against her leg. She reached back for it, taking it as a great roar sounded above her head. The hailstorm had begun in earnest. She glanced back and saw Belle's hand disappear as she quickly moved away from the onslaught of the spheres of ice which were already piling up against the steps.

Poppy clicked on the flashlight, shining it in the direction from which she thought the sound came. Tangles of cobwebs stretched between the floor beams. The softer earth toward the center of the ancient house had been pocked and hillocked by burrowing insects. *Oh well, Wondercrone. No need to worry about the knees, 'cause you're gonna be eaten alive by something before you ever stand up again.*

114

She crawled forward cautiously, shining the light around and behind each foundation pillar as she passed it. "Here girl . . . talk to Poppy." She whistled, but the sound was almost lost in the noise of the storm behind her. She neared what she thought must be the center of the house beside a mound of bricks where one of the old supports had given way and fallen. The light suddenly reflected from something, a piece of glass, Poppy thought. The amber glow winked out, then reappeared. It took Poppy a moment to realize she was looking straight into Kali's eye. The dog was so black she seemed to merge with the darkness around her.

"Kali . . . good dog. Good girl . . . what's the matter, girl? Tell Poppy what's wrong." Poppy moved with care, slowly. She reached forward and fear clutched her chest as something furry smacked her hand then slithered across her face, knocking her spectacles askew. *"Shit!"* She drew back, her breath coming in jerks. "What the hell was *that?"*

She straightened her glasses and shined the light toward the dog. *Dillworth, you dumbshit . . . why don't you just go ahead and die of fright? Your tombstone'll be a public curiosity. Here lies Poppy D. — R.I.P. Killed by the wag of a dog's tail.*

Kali was on her side, her tail thumping slow and weak against the earth. Poppy crawled closer. The dog's head was matted with dried blood and one eye was swollen shut. Poppy reached out her free hand and lightly touched the big dog's shoulder. "Is that it, girl? You just get hit on the head? Are you hurt anywhere else?" She moved her hand up and down the dog's body searching for other wounds. Kali's sides heaved and she tried to raise her head but fell weakly back as Poppy cautiously rolled her over to check the other side.

Finding no more visible damage, Poppy leaned her forehead against the dog's neck and murmured comforting words. Words which got away from her and turned into sobs. First of relief and then of grief and then for all the things she hadn't cried about in years. She realized the dog was struggling to rise. *Dillworth, you foolish old woman. Suck it up, girl. You're upsetting the dog, for Chrisake.*

Poppy removed her shirt and arranged Kali on it. She inched backward toward the steps, using the shirt as a sling to pull the dog with her as she went. As she neared her destination beneath the porch steps, Poppy felt the cold air from the hail kiss her naked skin. She turned and looked toward the opening.

"Hey! Papillon," Belle shouted, her head upside down as she lay on the porch and looked under. "Answer me, honey! Are you all right!"

"Yeah. I'm all right, but Kali's not. She's been hurt, but she's alive. C'mon down and help me lift her out."

Poppy heard someone scraping away the drift of hail beside the steps, then suddenly Belle's arms were around her bare shoulders. Poppy sniffed and said gruffly, "Let's get her up to the light. Can't make out how bad it is."

Seconds later they had lifted Kali onto the porch and placed her on the bench seat of the swing where Lovey hovered over her with the authority of one who had spent a lifetime of nursing, daily inspecting the wounds of humans. "Looks like a bullet wound to me, but I don't think it penetrated her skull.

Hard-headed old dog. Musta grazed it though. Bone's visible here over her eye."

While Lovey continued to minister to the dog, Poppy slipped into a shirt Pete handed her. She looked out across the yard, suddenly aware of her surroundings. Mounds and drifts of hail covered the area. The cedar trees near the porch had been stripped bare. The pungent odor of cedar sap rose around them on floating rivers of steam.

Belle clapped her hand to her forehead. "Juno — good lord." She hurried into the house. "I'll go get Juno."

Poppy inspected her knees. Nothing showed on the outside, but inside they felt as if someone had broken off a rusty knife somewhere behind each kneecap. She rubbed them as she looked out over the valley. Clouds of steam rose everywhere. Trees stood gaunt, many completely leafless, others still green but spare against the whitened landscape. It looked like a bad Stephen King movie. She half expected pterodactyls to come screeching over as great long-necked creatures rose from the river bottoms.

Poppy rubbed her glasses with the hem of Pete's shirt, then plopped them on her nose and waited for Belle and Juno to return. *Uh-oh, W.C.* Poppy's gaze came to rest on the Trooper. *Good thing we have insurance. What is it with us anyway? Every case we go on, we ruin a vehicle.* There didn't seem to be a space over an inch square where the hail hadn't pounded dents into the Isuzu's blue body.

The door burst open and Juno exploded onto the porch. *"Kali!"* she shrieked. "Kali-Kali-Kali." The big dog whimpered and tried to rise but Juno knelt and

117

clasped her arms around Kali. Her small shoulders shook as she sobbed into the dog's furry neck.

Poor old dog's had her share of blubbering females today, hasn't she, W.C.?

Belle covered them both with a light blanket. Juno sat up, her eyes wide. She wiped her nose on a tissue Belle handed her. "What's the matter with her, Belle? Where did you find her? Is Kali gonna be okay?"

"She'll be just fine as soon as we get the veterinarian to look at her head. She was under the house. Poppy heard her and went under there after her."

"But," Juno countered, not to be mollified, "what happened to her head? D'you think someone shot her?"

Poppy replied, "That's what Lovey says. She thinks Kali was just grazed, though. That the bullet just stunned her and she crawled under the house and passed out . . . I imagine the same thing that woke you from your nap brought Kali back to consciousness — the thunderclap that happened when the lightning struck that weathervane in the yard."

Poppy turned her attention to the weather as a blast of wind hit the house. It seemed the storm was now ready to begin again. "C'mon," she said, standing. "Let's get Kali in the Trooper and get on in to the vet's office." She opened the vehicle doors for the others and gazed out over the valley while the dog-loading was accomplished. The layers of steam had begun to swirl and dissipate beneath the pressure of the wind. They had just pulled away from the house when the raindrops came slanting in, drumming hard against the vehicle. The deluge began to fill the ditches and run across the road in places, darkening as it picked up the earth, hailstones carried on its crest like melting marshmallows on hot cocoa. Poppy drove carefully, her attention fully on the task at hand.

They finally arrived at the veterinarian's office and Poppy parked in front, greatly relieved to see other vehicles still there. Kali was taken swiftly into surgery and the two women and the girl sat, bedraggled, in the waiting room.

"I hope Mom's okay." Juno snuggled under Belle's arm.

Belle answered with a question. "She and Marsha will probably stay in Dallas until the storms pass, don't you think, Poppy?"

Poppy agreed, and said so, but she was ashamed of herself when she realized she hadn't even thought about the other women until now. The whole mystery surrounding Christine Jessup's death had been effectively driven from her mind by the adventure of finding Kali. Now she sat and silently mulled over all the angles again, shuffling once more through all those labelled folders on her imaginary desk. She arrived at no new conclusions and decided she was just too physically tired to think cogently about the mess.

Poppy was greatly relieved when the veterinarian's assistant motioned for them to follow him. They passed by cages of cats, dogs and one large rabbit. The young man patted Juno confidently on the shoulder. "Kali's going to be just fine, Juno. The x-rays don't show any damage. She's going to be better than new. She'll just have a little scar when the stitches come out."

Poppy was distracted by soft whining and yipping from a large cage over to one side at the back of the room. While Belle and Juno patted a very groggy Kali, Poppy watched a writhing mass of yellow puppies as they suckled, kicking and squealing and rooting each other out of the way. The mother dog was a fine yellow Labrador retriever, in shape, at least, like Kali, only more beautiful, in Poppy's eyes. Her light color made her features seem stronger. She raised her head and looked Poppy squarely in the eye, her blond brows knitted in a somehow fretful expression, her dark muzzle open, panting.

The leprechaun did his little trick inside of Poppy's chest. She walked closer, then knelt down on creaking knees and cautiously placed her hand flat against the cage by the puppies. The mother dog let her head drop slowly back to the mat, apparently unalarmed by Poppy's presence.

Poppy wriggled her fingers through the wire and touched the fuzzy back of one of the pups. She stroked the warm little body. The pup flopped over, tummy-side up. A lump swelled in Poppy's throat and something way down inside loosened and bloomed, uncurling in waves through her chest and abdomen. The pup made scratching motions with its back leg as Poppy's fingers tickled its ribcage. It suddenly righted itself and began to gnaw at her fingers, mock-furious as it swung its head from side to side, growling and tugging, its feet slipping against the mat. Then Poppy noticed its eyes. One was amber and the other was light blue. "Hey, little Fancy-Face. What happened to you anyway? Your folks have designer genes? Looks like you got the best of both of 'em."

The mother dog raised her head at the sound of Poppy's voice.

"She's our star boarder," said a voice at Poppy's elbow. "She was having some trouble feeding all those pups, so we're giving her a hand for a few weeks." The veterinarian, a plump young woman, knelt beside Poppy.

"How many pups did she have?" Poppy looked into the pen at the mass of tiny bodies.

"Sixteen."

"Whew." *No wonder she looks tired, W.C. Not enough pumps there to fill all those little tanks.*

The young woman continued, "We usually don't have pups this old in the whelping area. They're cuties, aren't they?"

Not deigning to answer the obvious, Poppy instead asked, "What's the matter with this one's eye?"

"Nothing, except for an aberration in the pigmentation. Her vision is normal, she just has an off-eye. It's a shame, too. She's probably the best pup in the litter except for that flaw. The owner will take a loss on her, if she's sold at all."

No. Not now, Dillworth. We got a job to do. Poppy gently pulled her fingers through the wire. She rose and squared her shoulders, willing the lump in her throat to go away. She looked up to see that Juno and Belle were ready to go. They followed the young man who carried Kali through the lessening rain and placed her on the back seat of the battle-scarred Trooper.

As they drove back to the camp, passing over the rapidly flowing Hermosa River, Poppy found herself once more wishing for a calm evening and a full night's sleep.

But thoughts of sleep quickly receded from Poppy's mind when Lovey and Pete met them at the front door of the farmhouse. "Poppy. You're not gonna believe this." Pete's Eve's apple bobbed in excitement. "They just found Tyrone Needham dead. Blew his brains out! Left a note. Admitted to killing Chris and embezzling from the Jessup estate. Whaddayou think about all that?"

Poppy sat heavily in the rocking chair. She had to have a lot more answers before she would know *what* she thought about that.

CHAPTER NINE
Poppy Goes Fishing

The next morning, after the passing of more rainstorms and a less than restful night, Poppy sat once more at the oval table in the farmhouse dining room. Pete and Lovey and Belle were clearing breakfast dishes from the table while Poppy concentrated on the pages of notes in her yellow tablet.

Lil and Marsha, safely home from Dallas, had left again for Pecan Valley to find out more about the banker's suicide and to see if a friend of Lil's could get them a copy of the note he left behind. Juno sat on the floor beside Poppy's chair patting the rapidly recuperating Kali.

Pete poked Poppy's shoulder. "Hey, Sherlock. Phone call for you." She pointed toward the kitchen doorway, where Lovey stood holding the receiver.

Poppy rose stiffly. Her whole bone structure felt as if she had been playing million-dollar quarterback behind an underpaid front line. She took the phone from Lovey and raised the instrument to her ear. "Dillworth here."

"Hey, Pops. T.J. Ballew. Howya doin'?"

"I've had better days, T.J. . . . You got something for me? Or is this just to let us know that Cleopatra misses her mamas?" Poppy saw Pete's expression but it was too late. The cat stuff had already got loose.

T.J. answered, her voice low and resonant. "Naw, Pops. I wouldn't want Belle to know, but I don't think this hussy of a cat misses *any*body. The reason I called was to let you in on what I've uncovered about Christine Jessup's family. Seems like preacher Emory Jessup, Chris's father, was having all kinds of money problems just before him and Chris's mother were killed in that crash."

"Really?"

"Yeah. As we all know, the Dallas real estate market's been in a pretty bad slump since the price of Texas oil bottomed out. And E.Z. Jessup had a big chunk tied up in some prime downtown office buildings. And then all that bad press about those TV preachers just about dried up the mail-ins for E.Z.'s television ministry. When the banks tightened up on credit, he just about went under. Word is that he was on a trip up to Tulsa to try to scare up some financing when he died. The B-word had even been bandied about . . . *bankruptcy*."

"So there may not be much of an estate left. Is that what you're saying?"

"My source in Dallas dried up on that. The trail left Dallas, she said, and all of the Jessup holdings are now consolidated and being handled by a guy named Tyrone Needham, who's the president of Pecan Valley State Bank."

"Thanks, T.J. As usual, you've done a good job. But, unless Needham can wheel and deal through a Ouija board, he's gonna need an assistant who's still in the land of the visible."

"Huh?"

"He shot himself yesterday. Rumor says he left a note admitting to Christine Jessup's murder and also mentioned the fact that he was helping himself to funds from her estate."

"Uh-oh . . . Well, Pops, does that mean y'all will be coming home soon?"

"Dunno, T.J. Maybe. You and Cleo getting along okay?"

"No problems, there. Pecker's getting a little cranky from being cooped up in her cage all the time. But that bird's *never* in a good mood if I sit a home that's owned by a cat. We're fine, really . . . Uh, Cleo did throw up once in your chair, Pops, but don't take it personal. I'm afraid she over-indulged herself on sausage pizza. She's okay now. I forgot how sneaky she is. I left the pizza box out on the kitchen cabinet. She ate four whole pieces. Licked the box clean. Didn't even leave a greasy spot . . .

Course there's a little greasy spot on your *chair,* but I'm gonna get it out before y'all get home."

"I don't think I want to know any more, T.J. I'll call before we leave, okay?"

"All right, Pops. Good luck." T.J. rang off and Poppy turned to Belle to relay T.J.'s information. The phone rang again, startling her. She reached for it.

"Dillworth here. I mean, Hallelujah Bend . . . Oh yeah. Hey, *Bubba!*" She nodded at Belle, pointing to the phone. "It's Bubba Swindell." She turned back to the phone. "Yeah, it's me. Good to hear your voice, son."

"I only have a minute or two, Poppy, but here goes. That specimen you sent me contained parts of a cicada. It also shows traces of human hair and scalp tissue. It was heavy with limestone particles. Where'd it come from?"

"It was mashed into a tree trunk on top of the cliff where Christine Jessup was last seen alive. The smudge of white from the limestone was how Belle found it."

"Maybe someone hit the Jessup woman on the head with a limestone rock, and maybe part of the rock hit the tree and the cicada," said Bubba. "Or maybe she was standing close to the tree and the rock ricocheted into it."

"Yeah . . . something like that." Poppy's thoughts were moving rapidly ahead. "Thanks, Bubba. Say howdy to Red, and tell her we'll be there when the birthing takes place. Keep us posted."

"Okay Poppy. Give my respects to Miz Stoner. I gotta go now and supervise the delivery of the academy's new helicopter. I just *love* my new job. It's good to be the *only* Swindell for a change. Listen, you need anything else, just call. So long, Poppy. Take care now."

Poppy cradled the phone and turned to the roomful of expectant faces. She spent some minutes filling them in on the recent developments. When she had satisfied most of their questions, she excused herself and took her notepad and the tape from the video camera into the recreation room. She inserted the tape into the V.C.R. and settled back to view it once more.

Poppy's mind was awash with possible scenarios about how the murder might have happened. She probably now had proof that Christine had indeed been murdered, but Tyrone Needham's suicide made the proof redundant.

Or did it?

And what of Gloria Needham, the banker's wife? How desperate was she to keep up appearances? And just how far had Tyrone Needham *been* under his wife's thumb? Could Gloria Needham have had anything to do with her husband's death? Poppy had seen the results of enough murder cases in her years with the Sheriff's Department to know that a woman, a mother, could commit many desperate acts in the name of misguided maternal protection, or even to protect social position.

And how did Lavon "Gunner" Gatling and her Sheriff husband fit into the big picture? Why had the Gunner been so interested in the banker on the morning of his death? Tyrone Needham *had* seemed worried and distracted when Poppy and the others had spoken to him in the bank parking lot, but no more so than any other harried husband and father of two very pretty and expensive daughters. But his demeanor had changed abruptly when he caught sight of Lavon Gatling.

Yeah, Wondercrone. The guy skittered. Remember? Big, tall, handsome, red-headed banker guys don't skitter unless they experience fear. Y'know, as in "afraid?"

And had it really been Lavon he was trying to duck — or had he seen the nefarious Boscos arrive in their shiny bubba-truck?

Poppy punched the buttons on the remote control, pausing now and again as the tape ran. The murder case at Red Rook Ranch had hinged on something she had missed on a tape, until it had been almost too late. She didn't intend for that to happen again. But this time there was no crow on a fencepost to catch her eye. The tape ended and nothing at all had jumped out at her. She rewound it and started it once more.

This time she viewed the tape more slowly, repeatedly pausing for stills. *Waitaminute. What's that?* She rewound it and clicked forward. There was something in that instant before Kali had hit the water when Juno and the dog played fetch, when Poppy was filming on the riverbank. She now caught a glimpse of something whiter than the rest of the river bottom. She couldn't make out what it was.

But she remembered another time when she had taped that same pool. She fast-forwarded until she saw Belle against the tree where they had found the cicada.

There. Aha! In her excitement Poppy stood and walked closer to the television screen, peering at the picture before her. She remembered standing there on the cliff and turning the camera down toward the river to pan the long pool where Juno had found Chris Jessup under the water. There it was. Something whiter than the rest of the bottom of the pool winked back at her.

The murder weapon, Fearless Tracker. There it is. A chunk of limestone that someone used to kill Chris. And then mashed the bug. And then did the most natural thing in the world. They threw it in the river. Poppy couldn't quite discern how large it was, but the rock had not been under the water long enough to become coated with grayish sediment like the smooth limestone shelf upon which it rested. It stood out like a hole in a window shade.

Should be easy enough to retrieve. Couldn't be very deep right there. "Oh shit," Poppy exclaimed as she remembered the way the river had looked the *last* time she had seen it. The river was running high in its banks; the storms had swelled it with a flood of whitish, muddy water. The calm river pools would be gone now, beneath a flood of debris from the hail. Broken limbs and leaves had roiled on the crest of the normally gentle river and anything which had been resting on the bottom of the "font" of Hallelujah Bend could be anywhere down river, or buried under tons of gravel.

Poppy sat dejectedly. She contemplated the vagaries of being a private investigator in Texas, where the weather could kill you quicker than the rednecks.

Belle appeared beside Poppy. "Lil and Marsha are back from town. They got a copy of the suicide note from Lil's friend at the courthouse. Come and see."

Poppy made herself stay and rewind the tape.

She retrieved it from the V.C.R. and stored it in her tote bag, tucking it in beside her holstered pistol. Who knew? It *could* become important.

She joined the other women on the front porch. She took the piece of paper Marsha extended and read it slowly. It had been handwritten on bank stationary. *I can no longer live with myself. I killed Christine Jessup. I pushed her into the river. I did it because she found out I embezzled money from the Jessup estate. She threatened to go to the authorities. May God forgive me. Signed — Tyrone M. Needham.*

The sight of Marsha, pale and shaken, reminded Poppy with a jolt that the death and apparent guilt of Tyrone Needham must have been doubly hard on the tall woman who now sat on the porch slumped dispiritedly beneath Lil's arm. He was family, after all.

Lil said, "I bet we never see one cent out of this whole mess . . . Poor Chris. All she wanted was to save the river. She really seemed to come to life for a while there — to be finding herself, finally . . . That *lowlife*."

Poppy's inner dialogue ran in a similar direction, but with a little different tack. *Yeah, W.C., the banker might've been a lowlife, but he didn't kill that girl, did he? Nopers . . . Note says he pushed her into the river. And we know someone hit her on the head with a rock. Which ain't zackly the same thing now, is it?* But why would a man about to die make a mistake like that? If he had been *forced* to write the confession? He might have done it on purpose in hopes of pointing to the real killer.

Poppy felt a sudden desire for solitude. She needed a few moments to exercise her stiff knees and clear her head. She expressed this to the women on the porch. "I think I'll take a pole and go down to the catfish ponds. Maybe catch a few for lunch. Might give me a chance to get my thoughts in order." For some reason she didn't quite understand, she wasn't yet ready to share her conclusions with her friends, not even with Belle.

Poppy walked past the place where just a few days ago the garden had stood in neat green rows. Now it was flattened, destroyed by the hailstorm. A few bare and broken cornstalks leaned crazily, trying to right themselves in the morning sunshine. The catfish empoundments were full and, just as she surmised, the fish, energized by all the fresh water, were eager and hungry. It was almost too easy. She'd been there less than fifteen minutes and the fish basket was already home to four channel-cats weighing about two pounds each. More than enough for lunch.

She twirled the cane pole, wrapping the line around it, and secured the hook. *Awright, Wondercrone. It's time to clean these beauties.* She hefted the wire basket, admiring the way the sun gleamed from the iridescent bellies of the fish, and carried them to the cleaning table. The job was about half done when the sound of an automobile caused her to look up.

Tom Ross Needham's red Porsche was coming up the drive toward the house. Poppy waved and he slowed, then stopped and backed up, turning onto the lane which led to the ponds. He stopped and neatly levered himself from the sleek car and strode quickly across the low dam. He carried a thick spiral notebook under his arm.

"I'm glad I found you alone, Ms. Dillworth. I need to talk to you." He stood awkwardly in front of Poppy, watching her as she cleaned the fish.

"And I'm glad you found me," Poppy answered. "Here, grab one of these and put those big hands to work." She smiled inwardly at her own cantankerousness. She watched with surprise as the young man lay the notebook aside and unhesitatingly grasped the largest of the slippery fish.

They worked in silence for a few minutes. Poppy was gratified to find that Tom Ross had, somewhere along the way, been instructed in the fine art of catfish cleaning. She watched as he efficiently bagged up the leavings and washed down the table, spraying water over it from the ancient red water hose by using his thumb to create a nozzle effect.

"Now then," Poppy said as she stuffed the creamy fillets into a Ziploc freezer bag, then dried her hands, offering Tom Ross one end of her towel. "Now then," she repeated. "What's up, son? That notebook yonder have anything to do with your trip out here this morning?"

"Yes ma'am, it does." He handed the notebook to Poppy. "It's Chris's journal. I've had it all along . . . I mean, I really did find it when I found the will. I'm sorry I lied about it. I couldn't bring myself to let anyone see it . . . until now."

"Why not?"

The tall young man standing before Poppy seemed to sag. He leaned heavily against the gate. "Well, it all started out when I was having an affair with Gunner." He glanced away from Poppy's scrutiny, obviously embarrassed at what he was about to reveal. "Well. See, when Mother and Lil first . . . I mean, when Mother first told me what she had discovered about herself —" He spoke slowly, seeming to try to find just the right words for something which had for him evidently been the source of great pain and confusion. "I was so angry with Mother that I guess I . . . wanted to distance myself in all ways. So I threw in with the lake crowd. Particularly Gunner." He looked at Poppy with a slightly defiant jut to his chin. "Lavon Gatling is pretty hard to resist when she decides she wants something."

We have no problem with that statement, do we, W.C.? Poppy relived the tiniest edge of the hot-waffle-cold-syrup feeling as Tom Ross continued.

"She wanted me to, uh —" He glanced up at Poppy, then away. "To . . . use my charms to distract Chris and get her to quit the river bunch and put her land up for sale." His shoulders dropped even lower as he continued. "But, when I got to know Chris, it all got mixed up . . . I didn't know *what* to do after a while. I fell in love with Chris and I just wanted Gunner to leave me alone. But she wouldn't. She kept pestering me. Said she'd have to handle it *herself* if I couldn't do it."

He looked searchingly at Poppy. She thought his expression was one of dismay and real confusion.

Tom Ross went on, "I didn't know *what* she meant by that. I guess I got a little crazy. You know how Gunner is. I thought she was gonna move in on Chris. You know? . . . I mean like *sexually* or something. Oh hell." He lowered his head. "I've just screwed everything up. I thought I could protect Chris and I failed. Now Uncle Ty's dead too . . ." His voice lowered and he swallowed hard. "I think the real killer is still walking around. Uncle Ty might have been skimming funds but I just can't believe he could kill anyone." He looked pleadingly at Poppy. "I don't think we know everything yet or even everyone who's involved in this mess."

Poppy made her decision about the young man's story and nodded agreement. "Me neither, Tom. For one thing, your Uncle Tyrone said in his note that he *pushed* Christine into the river. That tells me he didn't really do it, because *I* happen to know now how it *really* happened. And that ain't it."

Tom Ross looked up in amazement.

Poppy continued. "Is there anything in the journal we don't already know? Like maybe Chris's suspicions about Tyrone's embezzling?"

He handed the notebook to Poppy. "No. I don't think so. Only the stuff about me and Gunner. When I realized I was in love with Chris, I told her about that and she wrote some stuff about it." He looked at Poppy again with an appealing crease between his bronze-colored eyebrows. "I've got to go see Mother now. She's feeling pretty bad about Aunt Glo telling her not to come to the funeral. I've made up my mind to tell Mother I'm not going either. If they don't want my mother there — then they don't want me either."

Poppy nodded and patted the young man's arm. The old maternal grizzly bear inside of Poppy wanted to hug Tom Ross, to show him how proud she was, but Tom Ross drew himself up and stuck out his hand just in time to save Poppy from embarrassing both of them. "Maybe you can come up with some way to find out who really murdered Chris, Ms. Dillworth. I sure hope so."

Poppy solemnly shook his hand and watched as he went back to his car. She thought for a moment, then had a sudden glimmer of how the killer could be tempted out of hiding. She hurriedly gathered her bag of fish and her tackle box. The right person for the job she had in mind was the affable and courageous young reporter, Melvin Mossbacker.

CHAPTER TEN
Bait and Switch

The next morning began clear and the day warmed early. The cool front which had spawned the bad weather had moved on toward the Texas coast, leaving the earth naked and vulnerable under the relentless summer sun. Poppy woke before dawn, her stomach doing crazy things. She hoped that she and Melvin hadn't bitten off more than the both of them could handily spit out.

Poppy knew she was being a little unfair to Belle

by not confiding in her about the scheme she and Melvin had devised. But the thought of Belle in danger made her sick to her stomach. The thought of *herself* in danger was also unpleasant, but there was a good chance the whole scenario would flush the killer and bring the case to a conclusion.

After breakfast Poppy set her plan in motion by indicating she was restless and wanted to fish down by the river. Belle and Juno left for town on a mysterious errand. Poppy envied Belle's easy camaraderie with the girl. But then, Belle had raised daughters — *and* granddaughters — in that large part of her herstory before she had become the light of Poppy's life. A warm glow spread outward from the middle of her chest as she thought of how Belle was winning acceptance from her old friends. Even Pete was beginning to come around. Poppy suspected that Pete's recent change of heart concerning the two calico cats might have been Pete's odd way of making an apology to Belle.

Poppy stowed her fishing gear in the large red canoe she had dragged to the river bank from the shed by the cabin. She knelt in the ribbed bottom on complaining knees and leaned forward to let her weight slide the craft into the water. She noted that the river beyond the small oxbow lake was still running swiftly, but nothing like the flood of a few days ago. She dipped the wooden paddle, wetting its blade, then brought it to her nose, breathing in the smell of summers past.

A lazy eddy caught the canoe and moved it toward the bank again. She let it nose up beside the sturdy dock while she attached a feathered fly to her line. She could almost *feel* the pull of a hungry small-mouth bass. The anticipation of fishing had chased away her earlier shakiness. She looked at her watch. Half past nine. Melvin was late.

Nopers, W.C. Here he comes now. She watched the battered van circle and come to a stop by the cabin. Melvin got out, hitched up his denim pants, neatly tucking in the tail of his tee shirt, and waved to Poppy. He seemed confident and smiled widely as he neared the dock.

"Mornin', ma'am." He gestured toward the back seat of the canoe. "Mind if I join you?" He waded into the water, canvas shoes and all, and efficiently boarded as Poppy held the canoe steady against the dock. He seemed proficient in river etiquette and settled quickly onto his seat. He grasped his paddle, gesturing with it toward the river. "You do the fishing and I'll man the engines."

Poppy gladly accepted his offer. Chances like this didn't come around that often. She indicated a line of willows that hung close to the water's surface, and when they neared, she let the line sail from the tip of her favorite fly rod. The fly settled softly onto the glassy water at a place where the current lagged past dark pockets between the tree roots.

Melvin spoke quietly. "Well, ma'am. I got it all done. I called each one of the suspects, just like we talked about. If you're right about this — and I think you are — pretty soon one of those six people will rise to the bait."

Right on cue the water beneath the low willows exploded into action as a fish took Poppy's fly. "Wow! Lookit that mama dance!" Poppy set the hook and began the joyful task of reeling in her catch. As the fish ran to deeper water the line zipped and sang, then went slack when the fish shot into the air in a flashing leap not six feet from the canoe. Sun sparkled from the bass' silvery green sides as it danced on its tail, trying to shake the hook.

Poppy's heart thumped as she brought the finally defeated bass close enough for Melvin to use the net. She grasped the large fish firmly, and gently removed the feathered hook from its mouth. She held it up, admiring its shining muscular body. She spoke softly to the fish. "You did real good, little mama. Thank you." She looked at Melvin. "Didn't she, son? I bet she'd go four pounds, what do you think?"

He eyed the fish. "Yeah." He answered. "Real good for a small-mouth. I think the county record's only five-something."

Poppy steadied herself in the canoe, then lowered the fish gently back into the water. "G'on now. Git along — maybe we'll meet again some day." She released the fish and watched it as it hovered just beneath the surface, regaining its balance. She touched it lightly on the head. "G'on," she said, and tapped it. The fish shot downward and out of sight. "Whew . . . that was *fun!*"

Poppy washed her hands over the side of the canoe and dried them on her khaki shorts, suddenly conscious of the angular weight of the pistol in her pocket.

Something whizzed past her ear and ripped a line of bubbles in the water. Then she heard the *blooomp!* of the shot.

"Godamighty! Move that paddle, son! Somebody's *shooting* at us!" She threw her fly rod into the bottom of the canoe, scrambling for her paddle. The fight with the fish had caused them to drift into the channel where the little lake connected with the river. "Head for the river! Whoever it is, is up on the bluff. The river's our only chance."

The water erupted again in spurts as their assailant found the range. Shots echoed across the valley.

"*Oooph!*" Melvin said. "I've been hit . . ."

Poppy didn't dare turn to look. She shouted, "Is it bad, son?"

"It's not real bad. I can still paddle with one arm."

The river current caught them, surging against the canoe, pushing it rapidly down river. Soon the Hallelujah Bend was behind them and they heard no more shots.

"How bad is it, son?" Poppy looked around at Melvin.

"I'm pretty sure my arm's broken." His round face was drawn tight against the pain. "I can't make my elbow work." He rested his paddle across his knees as the river slowed and widened where it flowed over smoother terrain.

Poppy's mind was working at fast-forward speed. "Tie it up with this." She tugged her favorite purple bandanna from around her neck and extended it to him. "Far's I can remember, there's not even one decent place to beach until we get to the canoe livery at the state highway bridge." She looked back at her young partner again. "You gonna be okay?"

"Yeah. Bleeding's stopping now . . . Hey, I guess we got our answer, all right," he said between his teeth. "Somebody doesn't give a shit whether or not Chris wrote something incriminating in her journal. Did you see who it was?"

"Nope, not even a hint." Poppy rubbed her burning shoulder muscles. "I was digging water too hard. We got some action all right. Somebody took the bait, that's for sure. But, who the hell was it? I sure didn't expect anyone to react this early." *Great plan, W.C. Almost got us killed. Now we're sittin' here doing the Hiawatha down the river with a wounded man. Smooth move, Dickless Tracer. Now what?* Melvin was evidently right, Poppy thought, about the journal business. Someone had indeed become extremely irrational.

For some minutes they floated, between steep banks, prisoners of the river. Then the river narrowed, deepening where it ran faster between high bluffs, and they encountered a breathtaking stretch of white water where the land opened up again and the river became shallower. They dodged rocks and tree limbs and snags and finally floated free, once again on a more peaceful course. Poppy announced, "There it is. The bridge. Get ready, son. We'll run it up on the bank there just below the livery building."

They beached without incident and scrambled up the slippery bank toward the large warehouse-like building where the Hallelujah Bend canoes were stored.

Poppy heard a vehicle slide to a fast stop on the bridge above them. The hair on the back of her neck stood up. She knew immediately what had transpired. Their assailant had driven around to head them off at the bridge, but had been just a few seconds late.

Poppy pointed at the bridge and grabbed Melvin's good arm, urging him wordlessly toward the building. They gained the shadow of the warehouse just as the sound of the first shot echoed around them. They crawled past picnic tables and around the corner of the building. Poppy's heart lurched in fearful relief as she spotted Pete's old truck backed up to the open doors. Her old friend must have begun to ready the canoes for rental, now that the river was up.

"Pete's here. C'mon, let's get inside." Poppy moved quickly through the doors with Melvin close behind. She shouted, *"Pete!* You in here?" Poppy saw Pete flattened against the wall trying to peer out the window. *"Pete!* Get away from there!"

Shards and slivers of glass fell around them as a shot hit the window above Pete's head. Pete turned toward Poppy, her eyes round in surprise. "What the' blue hell is going on out there? Have the goddam rednecks finally lost it?"

"C'mon, Pete. Help me close this door!"

"Cain't." Pete wagged her head. "Truck's got it pinned tight. Won't move."

Poppy looked out the window past Pete and saw the movement of someone running through the trees. She grabbed Pete and motioned toward the rear of the large room. "Get outa sight. They're coming in after us!"

She turned to Melvin who was standing by the wall near the open doors. "Mel, you circle around behind and get up on the highway where they parked their vehicle. If the keys are in it, drive it on in to town. Get us some help, *quick!*"

Melvin looked at her, uncertain.

"Git!" Poppy commanded. "We'll be okay." She stuck her hand in her pocket and pulled out her pistol. "We'll hide, then get the drop on 'em. Besides," she added, "that busted wing of yours has put you out of commission."

He nodded grimly and slipped out the side door. Poppy grabbed Pete, who stood rigid by the window, and pushed her back between the stacks of canoes. She watched her disappear under one of them and then searched wildly for a position of concealment which would afford her some element of surprise when she got the chance to catch whoever it was with their guard down. Her gaze came to rest on the stacks of airless inner-tubes arrayed against the wall on wide shelves. She leaped for the crude ladder at the end of the shelves and barely managed to conceal herself behind the stacks when she heard a voice.

"Where are you, you decrepit old bag?" A menacing shadow appeared on the floor by the doors. "I know you're in there, too, Mossbacker." The voice quivered with sarcastic rage. "*Surely* you don't think I believe that crap about a *journal,* do you?"

Now Poppy knew the murderer's identity but her mind was still grappling with the awful truth. She could hardly accept how badly she had been fooled. She gripped her pistol tighter and watched in disbelief as Lavon Gatling stepped into the room and moved cautiously along the far wall, toward where

Pete was hidden. Poppy hoped Pete would remain quiet until Lavon came near enough for Poppy to push the stacks of inner tubes over on her.

The enraged woman kept up her derisive chiding as she peered into each stack of canoes. Soon Poppy would be forced to make a move. She couldn't let harm come to her old friend. She gripped her .38 Police Special and pointed it at the woman, who, under other circumstances, had made Poppy's heart thump in a very different way.

Another shadow spread across the doorway. "Lavon, you in there?" Sheriff Troy Gatling eased into the doorway of the building, his gun in his hand, omnipresent cigar in his mouth.

Poppy heard the Sheriff's wife mutter, "Goddam, where'd that fool come from?" Then Lavon Gatling shouted, "Yes, Troy. I'm in here, and if you know what's good for you, you'll go on back to town and let me take care of this business myself!"

"What business is that, Lavon?"

"The business that old dyke's been digging up about me and Chris Jessup. She thinks she can prove I killed her."

Troy Gatling moved closer, cigar hanging loosely. He asked in a hushed, halting voice. "You mean it's true about the Jessup girl's diary?" He continued in a hoarse whisper, "Did you kill her, Lavon?"

Lavon Gatling's laugh was heavy with irony. "Of course I did, you fool. While *you've* been out fishing with those idiot friends of yours, *I've* been building up an empire. Chris Jessup — and her father before her — wanted to destroy all my dreams." A smirk spread across her face. "I killed *him* too, you know. The preacher found out Tyrone and I were using his money on a real estate deal in Dallas."

The sheriff leaned against a support post and let his gun point at the floor. "Lavon — baby. You and Tyrone weren't . . ."

"Weren't what? Lovers? No, it was strictly business."

"Did you kill him, too?"

"Yes, you dimwit. I *had* to. I hold most of the paper on that damned bank. If it *fails* . . . well . . . That won't happen. I won't *let* it happen. And now that you know all this, you'd better help me get rid of these meddlers. They know too much. That is, you'll help me *if* you want to keep on smoking imported cigars and taking vacations in Hawaii."

"You've made a fool out of me, Lavon." The Sheriff spat out his cigar and ground it into the cement floor.

Lavon Gatling strode toward her husband and stood in front of him, her extended finger pressing his chest. The two of them were so close to Poppy she was afraid they would hear her breathing. "I've made a multi-millionaire out of you, Troy — Now stop sniveling and *help* me for once in your life — be a *man!*"

Troy Gatling stared into the gloom past Lavon and spoke leadenly. "All right, Lavon. But it'll have to look like an accident. I've got Mossbacker handcuffed out in the cruiser . . . I caught him on the road to town in your Jeep. When he told me what was going on out here, I couldn't believe it. Had to see for myself . . . I take it he also knows too much?"

"Correct," Lavon answered, looking surprised, Poppy thought, that Melvin was not still in the building.

"Okay. I'll go get him and bring him in here. Then we can set this place afire." The sheriff turned toward the door.

Awright, W.C. It's time. Poppy tensed her body, readying her knees and feet against the inner tubes. She shoved with all the strength she could muster.

What happened next was almost a blur. She saw Lavon raise her pistol and point it at her husband's back. Poppy couldn't believe it even as her eyes took in the fact that Lavon Gatling was going to kill her husband. The sheriff fell heavily as the noise of the shot drowned out the sound of the falling rubber tubes.

Lavon turned toward Poppy, scrabbling to rid herself of the tangled mass of tubes. Poppy shouted, "Don't try it! I've got a gun!"

Poppy rolled from the shelf and stood. She pointed the .38 at the sheriff's wife, her finger tensed tight against the trigger.

Bloomp!

Poppy jerked back in shock as a bullet found its target and Lavon Gatling's body spun to the side and crumpled to the floor.

Poppy looked at her pistol in dismay as Troy Gatling crawled toward his wife. Her knees trembled as she realized what had happened. It hadn't been Poppy's shot which had felled Lavon. Poppy had not fired her pistol. The *sheriff* had shot his wife.

Troy Gatling, a deep red stain spreading across his back, cradled his wife's lifeless body to him. "Oh, Lavon baby. Forgive me. You've killed us both, babe.

147

What did you do it for? Oh God. You shouldn'a done it."

Poppy saw Pete appear from under the canoe. She motioned for her to come near, pointing to her own pistol, then at the weapons on the floor. Pete nodded and walked quickly to the ruined couple. She retrieved the pistols and backed away.

Poppy leaned heavily against the counter. "Pete," she said loudly. "Go out there and use the Sheriff's radio to call for the ambulance and some deputies . . . I think this case is over."

CHAPTER ELEVEN
Shazam!

Many hours later, Poppy and the others sat in the shady yard of the farmhouse at Hallelujah Bend. The sun wallowed on the horizon, a flattened red globe, sending its late evening rays across the valley to splash against the purple building. The house seemed to glow with lavender energy, a comfortingly *lesbian* sort of feeling. Poppy was beginning to think that maybe she liked the paint job after all.

Poppy's chair was backed against the trunk of

the great pecan tree and Pete's was nearby. Belle sat on a stool beside Poppy, holding Poppy's hand. Poppy choked back a chuckle as Sophie and Sybyl used Pete's lap for a launching pad when Kali nosed a little too close. They lunged for the safety of the tree as Pete raised her hands palm-up and sent Belle a look that said, *Why me?*

Melvin, with his bandaged arm in a sling, sat close to Ralph, who was handsome and serious in his Ranger uniform. The others were gathered in a tight semicircle and Juno lay on her back in the grass kicking at the tire swing. They all listened to Poppy and Melvin and asked questions about the climactic events of the morning.

Lil said, "I suppose we'll just have to guess it was Gunner who came here searching for the will and shot at Kali, since you say she never mentioned it, Poppy. But I think the biggest surprise of all is finding out that Gunner killed Chris's parents. She must've done something to their airplane." She leaned forward, looking at Poppy. "Is that how you see it?"

"Yeah. Had to be. I should have put it together when we were at the Gatling's house and she was showing us her office. There was a photograph of her airplane with the Sheriff standing beside it. Now that I call it to mind, I remember seeing another airplane in the background, one with the word *Godspeed* across its nose . . . Yeppers, shoulda put it together then."

Belle looked at Poppy, an arch expression around her eyes. "As I recall, you were somewhat distracted at the time, Papillon." Belle squeezed her hand a little harder than Poppy thought was necessary, if comforting Poppy was Belle's true objective.

The syrup-and-waffle feeling in Poppy's abdomen had now been replaced by a sickly chill. She adroitly changed the subject. "Lil, what did you find out from your attorney? Did Sylvia give you *any* hope for this whole mess ever getting unravelled?"

"Yeah. She did, actually." Lil patted Marsha's hand and grinned over at Lovey as she continued. "Chris's will *is* valid and will stand up in court. But we don't know how much of the estate is left. We do know that at least a hundred thousand dollars is guaranteed by the bank's insurance and the deed to the Springs is unencumbered. So you'll have your Cronesnest after all, Lovey."

Lil turned back to Poppy. "Since the Sheriff is going to recover and has agreed to give testimony as to what really happened — there's a good chance now of saving the river. This whole thing should sway a lot of opinion our way. If it hadn't been for you, Poppy, Gunner would have gotten away with the whole thing. I don't know how we'll ever thank you."

Poppy felt Belle's hand leave her shoulder and saw her motion to Juno, who scrambled upright and ran from the yard.

Belle said, "Juno figured out a way . . . look."

Poppy turned to look in the direction Belle pointed and saw Juno, with Kali dancing around her, scurrying back across the grass carrying a lumpy bag. She placed it at Poppy's feet. Kali sat on her haunches, turning her head from side to side as Juno said, "Look, Poppy. Look inside."

151

Poppy leaned forward and peered into the mysterious bag. A pair of bright eyes looked back at her. One yellow-brown and one light blue.

"Fancy-face!" Poppy reached in and gathered the furry pup to her neck, trying to swallow past the lump in her throat.

Belle smiled at her. "She's yours, hon, if you want her."

The leprechaun in Poppy's heart jigged his way from atrium to ventricle and sent an almost enervating joy coursing through her body. She managed to find her voice. "Of *course* I want her! A dog. A *dog.* I gotta dog!" She buried her face in the squirming pup's plump, silky middle, hiding her tears from her friends.

The girl inside of Poppy ran around imaginary tracks, leaped from barn roofs into haystacks — *Captain Marvel* with a red towel tied around her neck. She screeched and whooped and skinned-the-cat on the very top rafter in the barn while her audience of cousins applauded far below. She ran and played and hunted with a big yellow dog at her side.

The sixty-five-year-old lesbian hugging the dog smiled through tears at her friends. "Thank you," she said in a husky voice. "With all my heart." And the girl inside shivered with joy as the puppy chewed on Poppy's ear.

About the Author

Dorothy Tell lives and writes in Texas with Ruth, her lifelong lover. She is still looking forward to her retirement (only *four* years now) when she will have all of her days to spend with Ruth and to write and read — And have long lunches with her daughter — And go to festivals — And visit with her mother and her sister — And go fishing with her granddaughter — And go back to Ruby Beach on Washington's Olympic Peninsula and look for agates — And go on a Vision Quest in New Mexico — And move to a house with a yard where she can *finally* have the big yellow dog she's wanted since she was a girl. And . . .

A few of the publications of
THE NAIAD PRESS, INC.
P.O. Box 10543 • Tallahassee, Florida 32302
Phone (904) 539-5965
Mail orders welcome. Please include 15% postage.

THE DAUGHTERS OF ARTEMIS by Lauren Wright Douglas.
240 pp. Third Caitlin Reece mystery. ISBN 0-941483-95-9 $8.95

CLEARWATER by Catherine Ennis. 176 pp. Romantic secrets
of a small Louisiana town. ISBN 0-941483-65-7 8.95

THE HALLELUJAH MURDERS by Dorothy Tell. 176 pp.
Second Poppy Dillworth mystery. ISBN 0-941483-88-6 8.95

ZETA BASE by Judith Alguire. 208 pp. Lesbian triangle
on a future Earth. ISBN 0-941483-94-0 9.95

SECOND CHANCE by Jackie Calhoun. 256 pp. Contemporary
Lesbian lives and loves. ISBN 0-941483-93-2 9.95

MURDER BY TRADITION by Katherine V. Forrest. 288 pp.
A Kate Delafield Mystery. 4th in a series. ISBN 0-941483-89-4 18.95

BENEDICTION by Diane Salvatore. 272 pp. Striking,
contemporary romantic novel. ISBN 0-941483-90-8 9.95

CALLING RAIN by Karen Marie Christa Minns. 240 pp.
Spellbinding, erotic love story ISBN 0-941483-87-8 9.95

BLACK IRIS by Jeane Harris. 192 pp. Caroline's hidden past . . .
ISBN 0-941483-68-1 8.95

TOUCHWOOD by Karin Kallmaker. 240 pp. Loving, May/
December romance. ISBN 0-941483-76-2 8.95

BAYOU CITY SECRETS by Deborah Powell. 224 pp. A Hollis
Carpenter mystery. First in a series. ISBN 0-941483-91-6 8.95

COP OUT by Claire McNab. 208 pp. 4th Det. Insp. Carol Ashton
mystery. ISBN 0-941483-84-3 8.95

LODESTAR by Phyllis Horn. 224 pp. Romantic, fast-moving
adventure. ISBN 0-941483-83-5 8.95

THE BEVERLY MALIBU by Katherine V. Forrest. 288 pp. A
Kate Delafield Mystery. 3rd in a series. (HC) ISBN 0-941483-47-9 16.95
Paperback ISBN 0-941483-48-7 9.95

THAT OLD STUDEBAKER by Lee Lynch. 272 pp. Andy's affair
with Regina and her attachment to her beloved car.
ISBN 0-941483-82-7 9.95

PASSION'S LEGACY by Lori Paige. 224 pp. Sarah is swept into
the arms of Augusta Pym in this delightful historical romance.
ISBN 0-941483-81-9 8.95

THE PROVIDENCE FILE by Amanda Kyle Williams. 256 pp.
Second espionage thriller featuring lesbian agent Madison McGuire
ISBN 0-941483-92-4   8.95

I LEFT MY HEART by Jaye Maiman. 320 pp. A Robin Miller
Mystery. First in a series.   ISBN 0-941483-72-X   9.95

THE PRICE OF SALT by Patricia Highsmith (writing as Claire
Morgan). 288 pp. Classic lesbian novel, first issued in 1952 . . .
acknowledged by its author under her own, very famous, name.
ISBN 1-56280-003-5   8.95

SIDE BY SIDE by Isabel Miller. 256 pp. From beloved author of
Patience and Sarah.   ISBN 0-941483-77-0   8.95

SOUTHBOUND by Sheila Ortiz Taylor. 240 pp. Hilarious sequel
to *Faultline.*   ISBN 0-941483-78-9   8.95

STAYING POWER: LONG TERM LESBIAN COUPLES
by Susan E. Johnson. 352 pp. Joys of coupledom.
ISBN 0-941-483-75-4   12.95

SLICK by Camarin Grae. 304 pp. Exotic, erotic adventure.
ISBN 0-941483-74-6   9.95

NINTH LIFE by Lauren Wright Douglas. 256 pp. A Caitlin
Reece mystery. 2nd in a series.   ISBN 0-941483-50-9   8.95

PLAYERS by Robbi Sommers. 192 pp. Sizzling, erotic novel.
ISBN 0-941483-73-8   8.95

MURDER AT RED ROOK RANCH by Dorothy Tell. 224 pp.
First Poppy Dillworth adventure.   ISBN 0-941483-80-0   8.95

LESBIAN SURVIVAL MANUAL by Rhonda Dicksion.
112 pp. Cartoons!   ISBN 0-941483-71-1   8.95

A ROOM FULL OF WOMEN by Elisabeth Nonas. 256 pp.
Contemporary Lesbian lives.   ISBN 0-941483-69-X   8.95

MURDER IS RELATIVE by Karen Saum. 256 pp. The first
Brigid Donovan mystery.   ISBN 0-941483-70-3   8.95

PRIORITIES by Lynda Lyons 288 pp. Science fiction with
a twist.   ISBN 0-941483-66-5   8.95

THEME FOR DIVERSE INSTRUMENTS by Jane Rule. 208
pp. Powerful romantic lesbian stories.   ISBN 0-941483-63-0   8.95

LESBIAN QUERIES by Hertz & Ertman. 112 pp. The questions
you were too embarrassed to ask.   ISBN 0-941483-67-3   8.95

CLUB 12 by Amanda Kyle Williams. 288 pp. Espionage thriller
featuring a lesbian agent!   ISBN 0-941483-64-9   8.95

DEATH DOWN UNDER by Claire McNab. 240 pp. 3rd Det.
Insp. Carol Ashton mystery.   ISBN 0-941483-39-8   8.95

MONTANA FEATHERS by Penny Hayes. 256 pp. Vivian and
Elizabeth find love in frontier Montana.   ISBN 0-941483-61-4   8.95

CHESAPEAKE PROJECT by Phyllis Horn. 304 pp. Jessie &
Meredith in perilous adventure.   ISBN 0-941483-58-4   8.95

LIFESTYLES by Jackie Calhoun. 224 pp. Contemporary Lesbian
lives and loves.   ISBN 0-941483-57-6   8.95

VIRAGO by Karen Marie Christa Minns. 208 pp. Darsen has
chosen Ginny.   ISBN 0-941483-56-8   8.95

WILDERNESS TREK by Dorothy Tell. 192 pp. Six women on
vacation learning "new" skills.   ISBN 0-941483-60-6   8.95

MURDER BY THE BOOK by Pat Welch. 256 pp. A Helen
Black Mystery. First in a series.   ISBN 0-941483-59-2   8.95

BERRIGAN by Vicki P. McConnell. 176 pp. Youthful Lesbian —
romantic, idealistic Berrigan.   ISBN 0-941483-55-X   8.95

LESBIANS IN GERMANY by Lillian Faderman & B. Eriksson.
128 pp. Fiction, poetry, essays.   ISBN 0-941483-62-2   8.95

THERE'S SOMETHING I'VE BEEN MEANING TO TELL
YOU Ed. by Loralee MacPike. 288 pp. Gay men and lesbians
coming out to their children.   ISBN 0-941483-44-4   9.95
                                         ISBN 0-941483-54-1   16.95

LIFTING BELLY by Gertrude Stein. Ed. by Rebecca Mark. 104
pp. Erotic poetry.   ISBN 0-941483-51-7   8.95
                                         ISBN 0-941483-53-3   14.95

ROSE PENSKI by Roz Perry. 192 pp. Adult lovers in a long-term
relationship.   ISBN 0-941483-37-1   8.95

AFTER THE FIRE by Jane Rule. 256 pp. Warm, human novel
by this incomparable author.   ISBN 0-941483-45-2   8.95

SUE SLATE, PRIVATE EYE by Lee Lynch. 176 pp. The gay
folk of Peacock Alley are all cats.   ISBN 0-941483-52-5   8.95

CHRIS by Randy Salem. 224 pp. Golden oldie. Handsome Chris
and her adventures.   ISBN 0-941483-42-8   8.95

THREE WOMEN by March Hastings. 232 pp. Golden oldie. A
triangle among wealthy sophisticates.   ISBN 0-941483-43-6   8.95

RICE AND BEANS by Valeria Taylor. 232 pp. Love and
romance on poverty row.   ISBN 0-941483-41-X   8.95

PLEASURES by Robbi Sommers. 204 pp. Unprecedented
eroticism.   ISBN 0-941483-49-5   8.95

EDGEWISE by Camarin Grae. 372 pp. Spellbinding
adventure.   ISBN 0-941483-19-3   9.95

FATAL REUNION by Claire McNab. 224 pp. 2nd Det. Inspec.
Carol Ashton mystery.   ISBN 0-941483-40-1   8.95

KEEP TO ME STRANGER by Sarah Aldridge. 372 pp. Romance
set in a department store dynasty.   ISBN 0-941483-38-X   9.95

HEARTSCAPE by Sue Gambill. 204 pp. American lesbian in
Portugal. ISBN 0-941483-33-9 8.95

IN THE BLOOD by Lauren Wright Douglas. 252 pp. Lesbian
science fiction adventure fantasy ISBN 0-941483-22-3 8.95

THE BEE'S KISS by Shirley Verel. 216 pp. Delicate, delicious
romance. ISBN 0-941483-36-3 8.95

RAGING MOTHER MOUNTAIN by Pat Emmerson. 264 pp.
Furosa Firechild's adventures in Wonderland. ISBN 0-941483-35-5 8.95

IN EVERY PORT by Karin Kallmaker. 228 pp. Jessica's sexy,
adventuresome travels. ISBN 0-941483-37-7 8.95

OF LOVE AND GLORY by Evelyn Kennedy. 192 pp. Exciting
WWII romance. ISBN 0-941483-32-0 8.95

CLICKING STONES by Nancy Tyler Glenn. 288 pp. Love
transcending time. ISBN 0-941483-31-2 9.95

SURVIVING SISTERS by Gail Pass. 252 pp. Powerful love
story. ISBN 0-941483-16-9 8.95

SOUTH OF THE LINE by Catherine Ennis. 216 pp. Civil War
adventure. ISBN 0-941483-29-0 8.95

WOMAN PLUS WOMAN by Dolores Klaich. 300 pp. Supurb
Lesbian overview. ISBN 0-941483-28-2 9.95

SLOW DANCING AT MISS POLLY'S by Sheila Ortiz Taylor.
96 pp. Lesbian Poetry ISBN 0-941483-30-4 7.95

DOUBLE DAUGHTER by Vicki P. McConnell. 216 pp. A Nyla
Wade Mystery, third in the series. ISBN 0-941483-26-6 8.95

HEAVY GILT by Delores Klaich. 192 pp. Lesbian detective/
disappearing homophobes/upper class gay society.

ISBN 0-941483-25-8 8.95

THE FINER GRAIN by Denise Ohio. 216 pp. Brilliant young
college lesbian novel. ISBN 0-941483-11-8 8.95

THE AMAZON TRAIL by Lee Lynch. 216 pp. Life, travel & lore
of famous lesbian author. ISBN 0-941483-27-4 8.95

HIGH CONTRAST by Jessie Lattimore. 264 pp. Women of the
Crystal Palace. ISBN 0-941483-17-7 8.95

OCTOBER OBSESSION by Meredith More. Josie's rich, secret
Lesbian life. ISBN 0-941483-18-5 8.95

LESBIAN CROSSROADS by Ruth Baetz. 276 pp. Contemporary
Lesbian lives. ISBN 0-941483-21-5 9.95

BEFORE STONEWALL: THE MAKING OF A GAY AND
LESBIAN COMMUNITY by Andrea Weiss & Greta Schiller.
96 pp., 25 illus. ISBN 0-941483-20-7 7.95

WE WALK THE BACK OF THE TIGER by Patricia A. Murphy.
192 pp. Romantic Lesbian novel/beginning women's movement.
ISBN 0-941483-13-4   8.95

SUNDAY'S CHILD by Joyce Bright. 216 pp. Lesbian athletics, at
last the novel about sports.   ISBN 0-941483-12-6   8.95

OSTEN'S BAY by Zenobia N. Vole. 204 pp. Sizzling adventure
romance set on Bonaire.   ISBN 0-941483-15-0   8.95

LESSONS IN MURDER by Claire McNab. 216 pp. 1st Det. Inspec.
Carol Ashton mystery — erotic tension!.   ISBN 0-941483-14-2   8.95

YELLOWTHROAT by Penny Hayes. 240 pp. Margarita, bandit,
kidnaps Julia.   ISBN 0-941483-10-X   8.95

SAPPHISTRY: THE BOOK OF LESBIAN SEXUALITY by
Pat Califia. 3d edition, revised. 208 pp.   ISBN 0-941483-24-X   8.95

CHERISHED LOVE by Evelyn Kennedy. 192 pp. Erotic
Lesbian love story.   ISBN 0-941483-08-8   8.95

LAST SEPTEMBER by Helen R. Hull. 208 pp. Six stories & a
glorious novella.   ISBN 0-941483-09-6   8.95

THE SECRET IN THE BIRD by Camarin Grae. 312 pp. Striking,
psychological suspense novel.   ISBN 0-941483-05-3   8.95

TO THE LIGHTNING by Catherine Ennis. 208 pp. Romantic
Lesbian 'Robinson Crusoe' adventure.   ISBN 0-941483-06-1   8.95

THE OTHER SIDE OF VENUS by Shirley Verel. 224 pp.
Luminous, romantic love story.   ISBN 0-941483-07-X   8.95

DREAMS AND SWORDS by Katherine V. Forrest. 192 pp.
Romantic, erotic, imaginative stories.   ISBN 0-941483-03-7   8.95

MEMORY BOARD by Jane Rule. 336 pp. Memorable novel
about an aging Lesbian couple.   ISBN 0-941483-02-9   9.95

THE ALWAYS ANONYMOUS BEAST by Lauren Wright
Douglas. 224 pp. A Caitlin Reece mystery. First in a series.
ISBN 0-941483-04-5   8.95

SEARCHING FOR SPRING by Patricia A. Murphy. 224 pp.
Novel about the recovery of love.   ISBN 0-941483-00-2   8.95

DUSTY'S QUEEN OF HEARTS DINER by Lee Lynch. 240 pp.
Romantic blue-collar novel.   ISBN 0-941483-01-0   8.95

PARENTS MATTER by Ann Muller. 240 pp. Parents'
relationships with Lesbian daughters and gay sons.
ISBN 0-930044-91-6   9.95

THE PEARLS by Shelley Smith. 176 pp. Passion and fun in
the Caribbean sun.   ISBN 0-930044-93-2   7.95

MAGDALENA by Sarah Aldridge. 352 pp. Epic Lesbian novel
set on three continents.   ISBN 0-930044-99-1   8.95

THE BLACK AND WHITE OF IT by Ann Allen Shockley.
144 pp. Short stories.   ISBN 0-930044-96-7   7.95

SAY JESUS AND COME TO ME by Ann Allen Shockley. 288
pp. Contemporary romance.   ISBN 0-930044-98-3   8.95

LOVING HER by Ann Allen Shockley. 192 pp. Romantic love
story.   ISBN 0-930044-97-5   7.95

MURDER AT THE NIGHTWOOD BAR by Katherine V.
Forrest. 240 pp. A Kate Delafield mystery. Second in a series.
    ISBN 0-930044-92-4   8.95

ZOE'S BOOK by Gail Pass. 224 pp. Passionate, obsessive love
story.   ISBN 0-930044-95-9   7.95

WINGED DANCER by Camarin Grae. 228 pp. Erotic Lesbian
adventure story.   ISBN 0-930044-88-6   8.95

PAZ by Camarin Grae. 336 pp. Romantic Lesbian adventurer
with the power to change the world.   ISBN 0-930044-89-4   8.95

SOUL SNATCHER by Camarin Grae. 224 pp. A puzzle, an
adventure, a mystery — Lesbian romance.   ISBN 0-930044-90-8   8.95

THE LOVE OF GOOD WOMEN by Isabel Miller. 224 pp.
Long-awaited new novel by the author of the beloved *Patience
and Sarah.*   ISBN 0-930044-81-9   8.95

THE HOUSE AT PELHAM FALLS by Brenda Weathers. 240
pp. Suspenseful Lesbian ghost story.   ISBN 0-930044-79-7   7.95

HOME IN YOUR HANDS by Lee Lynch. 240 pp. More stories
from the author of *Old Dyke Tales.*   ISBN 0-930044-80-0   7.95

EACH HAND A MAP by Anita Skeen. 112 pp. Real-life poems
that touch us all.   ISBN 0-930044-82-7   6.95

SURPLUS by Sylvia Stevenson. 342 pp. A classic early Lesbian
novel.   ISBN 0-930044-78-9   7.95

PEMBROKE PARK by Michelle Martin. 256 pp. Derring-do
and daring romance in Regency England.   ISBN 0-930044-77-0   7.95

THE LONG TRAIL by Penny Hayes. 248 pp. Vivid adventures
of two women in love in the old west.   ISBN 0-930044-76-2   8.95

HORIZON OF THE HEART by Shelley Smith. 192 pp. Hot
romance in summertime New England.   ISBN 0-930044-75-4   7.95

AN EMERGENCE OF GREEN by Katherine V. Forrest. 288
pp. Powerful novel of sexual discovery.   ISBN 0-930044-69-X   9.95

THE LESBIAN PERIODICALS INDEX edited by Claire
Potter. 432 pp. Author & subject index.   ISBN 0-930044-74-6   29.95

DESERT OF THE HEART by Jane Rule. 224 pp. A classic;
basis for the movie *Desert Hearts*.   ISBN 0-930044-73-8   8.95

SPRING FORWARD/FALL BACK by Sheila Ortiz Taylor.
288 pp. Literary novel of timeless love.   ISBN 0-930044-70-3   7.95

FOR KEEPS by Elisabeth Nonas. 144 pp. Contemporary novel
about losing and finding love.   ISBN 0-930044-71-1   7.95

TORCHLIGHT TO VALHALLA by Gale Wilhelm. 128 pp.
Classic novel by a great Lesbian writer.   ISBN 0-930044-68-1   7.95

LESBIAN NUNS: BREAKING SILENCE edited by Rosemary
Curb and Nancy Manahan. 432 pp. Unprecedented autobiographies
of religious life.   ISBN 0-930044-62-2   9.95

THE SWASHBUCKLER by Lee Lynch. 288 pp. Colorful novel
set in Greenwich Village in the sixties.   ISBN 0-930044-66-5   8.95

MISFORTUNE'S FRIEND by Sarah Aldridge. 320 pp. Histori-
cal Lesbian novel set on two continents.   ISBN 0-930044-67-3   7.95

A STUDIO OF ONE'S OWN by Ann Stokes. Edited by
Dolores Klaich. 128 pp. Autobiography.   ISBN 0-930044-64-9   7.95

SEX VARIANT WOMEN IN LITERATURE by Jeannette
Howard Foster. 448 pp. Literary history.   ISBN 0-930044-65-7   8.95

A HOT-EYED MODERATE by Jane Rule. 252 pp. Hard-hitting
essays on gay life; writing; art.   ISBN 0-930044-57-6   7.95

INLAND PASSAGE AND OTHER STORIES by Jane Rule.
288 pp. Wide-ranging new collection.   ISBN 0-930044-56-8   7.95

WE TOO ARE DRIFTING by Gale Wilhelm. 128 pp. Timeless
Lesbian novel, a masterpiece.   ISBN 0-930044-61-4   6.95

AMATEUR CITY by Katherine V. Forrest. 224 pp. A Kate
Delafield mystery. First in a series.   ISBN 0-930044-55-X   8.95

THE SOPHIE HOROWITZ STORY by Sarah Schulman. 176
pp. Engaging novel of madcap intrigue.   ISBN 0-930044-54-1   7.95

THE BURNTON WIDOWS by Vickie P. McConnell. 272 pp. A
Nyla Wade mystery, second in the series.   ISBN 0-930044-52-5   7.95

OLD DYKE TALES by Lee Lynch. 224 pp. Extraordinary
stories of our diverse Lesbian lives.   ISBN 0-930044-51-7   8.95

DAUGHTERS OF A CORAL DAWN by Katherine V. Forrest.
240 pp. Novel set in a Lesbian new world.   ISBN 0-930044-50-9   8.95

AGAINST THE SEASON by Jane Rule. 224 pp. Luminous,
complex novel of interrelationships.   ISBN 0-930044-48-7   8.95

LOVERS IN THE PRESENT AFTERNOON by Kathleen
Fleming. 288 pp. A novel about recovery and growth.
                    ISBN 0-930044-46-0   8.95

TOOTHPICK HOUSE by Lee Lynch. 264 pp. Love between
two Lesbians of different classes.   ISBN 0-930044-45-2   7.95

MADAME AURORA by Sarah Aldridge. 256 pp. Historical
novel featuring a charismatic "seer."   ISBN 0-930044-44-4   7.95

CURIOUS WINE by Katherine V. Forrest. 176 pp. Passionate
Lesbian love story, a best-seller.   ISBN 0-930044-43-6   8.95

BLACK LESBIAN IN WHITE AMERICA by Anita Cornwell.
141 pp. Stories, essays, autobiography.   ISBN 0-930044-41-X   7.95

CONTRACT WITH THE WORLD by Jane Rule. 340 pp.
Powerful, panoramic novel of gay life.   ISBN 0-930044-28-2   9.95

MRS. PORTER'S LETTER by Vicki P. McConnell. 224 pp.
The first Nyla Wade mystery.   ISBN 0-930044-29-0   7.95

TO THE CLEVELAND STATION by Carol Anne Douglas.
192 pp. Interracial Lesbian love story.   ISBN 0-930044-27-4   6.95

THE NESTING PLACE by Sarah Aldridge. 224 pp. A
three-woman triangle — love conquers all! ISBN 0-930044-26-6   7.95

THIS IS NOT FOR YOU by Jane Rule. 284 pp. A letter to a
beloved is also an intricate novel.   ISBN 0-930044-25-8   8.95

FAULTLINE by Sheila Ortiz Taylor. 140 pp. Warm, funny,
literate story of a startling family.   ISBN 0-930044-24-X   6.95

ANNA'S COUNTRY by Elizabeth Lang. 208 pp. A woman
finds her Lesbian identity.   ISBN 0-930044-19-3   8.95

PRISM by Valerie Taylor. 158 pp. A love affair between two
women in their sixties.   ISBN 0-930044-18-5   6.95

THE MARQUISE AND THE NOVICE by Victoria Ramstetter.
108 pp. A Lesbian Gothic novel.   ISBN 0-930044-16-9   6.95

OUTLANDER by Jane Rule. 207 pp. Short stories and essays
by one of our finest writers.   ISBN 0-930044-17-7   8.95

ALL TRUE LOVERS by Sarah Aldridge. 292 pp. Romantic
novel set in the 1930s and 1940s.   ISBN 0-930044-10-X   8.95

A WOMAN APPEARED TO ME by Renee Vivien. 65 pp. A
classic; translated by Jeannette H. Foster. ISBN 0-930044-06-1   5.00

CYTHEREA'S BREATH by Sarah Aldridge. 240 pp. Romantic
novel about women's entrance into medicine.
                                           ISBN 0-930044-02-9   6.95

TOTTIE by Sarah Aldridge. 181 pp. Lesbian romance in the
turmoil of the sixties.   ISBN 0-930044-01-0   6.95

THE LATECOMER by Sarah Aldridge. 107 pp. A delicate love
story.   ISBN 0-930044-00-2   6.95

ODD GIRL OUT by Ann Bannon.   ISBN 0-930044-83-5   5.95
I AM A WOMAN 84-3; WOMEN IN THE SHADOWS 85-1;   each
JOURNEY TO A WOMAN 86-X; BEEBO BRINKER 87-8. Golden
oldies about life in Greenwich Village.
JOURNEY TO FULFILLMENT, A WORLD WITHOUT MEN, and   3.95
RETURN TO LESBOS. All by Valerie Taylor   each

These are just a few of the many Naiad Press titles — we are the oldest and
largest lesbian/feminist publishing company in the world. Please request a
complete catalog. We offer personal service; we encourage and welcome direct
mail orders from individuals who have limited access to bookstores carrying
our publications.